TIME GHOST

OTHER BOOKS BY
Welwyn Wilton Katz

OUT OF THE DARK
COME LIKE SHADOWS
WHALESINGER
THE THIRD MAGIC
FALSE FACE
SUN GOD, MOON WITCH
WITCHERY HILL
THE PROPHECY OF TAU RIDOO

TIME
GHOST

WELWYN WILTON KATZ

A GROUNDWOOD BOOK

DOUGLAS & McINTYRE

TORONTO VANCOUVER

Groundwood Books / Douglas & McIntyre Ltd.
585 Bloor Street West
Toronto, Ontario M6G 1K5

The publisher gratefully acknowledges the assistance of the Canada
Council and the Ontario Arts Council.

Canadian Cataloguing in Publication Data

Katz, Welwyn
Time ghost

"A Groundwood book".
ISBN 0-88899-275-0

I. Title.

PS8571.A889T555 1996   jC813'.54   C96-931904-5
PZ7.K38Ti 1996

Cover illustration by Ted Nasmith
Text decorations by Martin Springett
Design by Michael Solomon
Printed and bound in Canada

For my daughter,
Meredith Allison Katz,
who at age nine asked the right question

Chapter One

"BUT you don't get it, Dani!" Sara wailed. "She's going to make me and Karl go with her! She acts like it's a treat. But who besides Grandma would want to go to the North Pole?"

Danielle's brown eyes sparkled. "Me!"

"But there's nothing up there. It's just one big emptiness. No cineboxes, no rollergyms, no blockbuildings like this one—"

Dramatically Sara waved her hand around Dani's bedroom, setting the hammock they were lying in swinging. It was a beautiful room, Sara thought. The walls were painted neon pink and the ceiling purple, and the hammock that hung from two hooks in the ceiling was a lovely iridescent blue. The bed was out of sight now, folded away into the wall, but Sara had slept over just last week and she knew that Dani had brand-new shiny blue bedding to match the hammock. Not like her own plain white sheets, or that horrible coverlet with its zillions of hooked yellow tufts that Sara pulled out one by one whenever she couldn't get to sleep.

Sara looked at the space where Dani's bed had been, envying her the giant computer screen that popped up whenever the bed was folded away, and the light-pen she'd been using to draw a picture of a horse before Sara had burst in. Dani was crazy about horses, even though she had never seen a live one. She had two holographs, one of a running stallion and the other of a mare and her colt, in the niches that were shaped and positioned exactly like the old-fashioned windows in Sara's grand-mother's house. Sara liked the holographs a lot better than the never-changing shimmer of Ottawa concrete that was the only view behind the curtains in her room at Grandma's house. She mostly kept them closed. Danielle could change the holographs whenever she wanted. All she had to do was tell her computer.

"Your place is a lot nicer than a blockbuilding like this one," Dani said. "It's not all closed in, and you have a lot more room. Your grandma's lucky to have a real house, even if you don't think so."

It was an old argument. Sara was too impatient to take Dani up on it. "But the North Pole!" she groaned. "Just Grandma and Karl and me!"

"Why does your grandma want you to go with her? What's she going for, anyway?"

"A Greysuit's going to try drilling for oil in the Arctic Ocean. And you know Grandma."

"Everybody knows Mrs. G and her Greysuits," Dani-elle answered with a knowing nod.

"Greysuits" was Grandma's name for the wealthy peo-ple who, she said, ran the world. Gwyneth Green had been a Supreme Court justice. She had stayed on the bench for ten years, and then, to everyone's surprise, she had faxed the prime minister, hung up her judge's wig and her robes, and walked out of her office to become the chief legal adviser to a save-the-world group called Grassroots. She didn't sit behind a desk, though. "Did that for too long already," she always said. *Now* what she did was go out and cause trouble.

Sara could hardly remember a time when her grand-mother's name and photograph had not been plastered all over the televids. Demonstrations, sit-ins, Save the Boreal Forest marches, lawsuits: if it wasn't one embarrassing thing, it was another. Sara's parents said Grandma had descended into her second childhood, but even they could not find fault with her legal abilities. No matter how annoying she was to the Greysuits, never once had anyone been able to find a legal way to put a stop to her activities.

It had felt like a betrayal when Sara's parents had gone off to a symposium on Luna One, sending her and Karl to live with Grandma for the year. Sara still couldn't understand it. How could they think what they did about Grandma and then go and send their kids to live with her? Sara would have preferred living with Dani, though it would have been crowded, or even going to Luna One with Mom and Dad, but nothing she wanted seemed to matter to her parents these days. There was room in the space shuttle only for the scientists, they said, adding things like "It'll be nice for you to get to know your grandmother," and "Blood is thicker than water, you know." A stupid thing for a pair of microbiologists to say, Sara still thought. The whole thing was stupid.

It had been six months since Sara had seen her parents except via telesat, six months of living in an old-fashioned house with a grandmother who lived in the past and wanted everyone else to live there, too. The only thing good about it was that Grandma's house was close enough that Sara hadn't had to change schools, and so she still got to see Dani. And now that it was summer, they spent most of every day together.

"When's Mrs. G taking you?" Dani said.

"Oh, she gave us lots of notice, as usual. I mean, we're only going to the North Pole, right? Why should we have to know more than a day ahead?"

"You mean you're going tomorrow?"

9

Sara nodded, grimacing. "I was *supposed* to be second skip in the roller tournament on Friday. And it's my birthday the day after tomorrow. We were going to have a party, but what does that matter to Grandma?"

"You could have a party at the North Pole," Dani said. "How many kids get to turn twelve at the North Pole?"

"Dani! There'll just be me and Karl and Grandma! What kind of a party is that? And the North Pole! That horrible empty place, nothing to do and no one to talk to. . . . I'll die of loneliness up there. Or maybe Karl will kill me before that. He tells me at least six times a day that he wants to."

"Brothers!" Dani said sympathetically. "Joshua is just as bad. Maybe that's why he and Karl are best friends. They have their meanness in common."

"At least with Josh you're okay as long as you stay out of his way while he does his experiments. With Karl, all I have to do is *breathe*!"

"Well, Josh is always doing his stupid experiments," Dani said, "and I can't stay out of his way all the time. Right now he's doing some big project about time, and there are chronometers and old-fashioned clocks everywhere I go, except in here."

"Tell me about it," Sara said grimly. "I saw them on my way in."

"Did he yell at you, too?"

"I just bent over to look at an old clock with handles. I just looked. That was all."

"Do you know what, Sara? Sometimes I get so sick of this place, a box with four tiny rooms—and nowhere to be by myself except in here—"

"At least you can make this room whatever you want it to be. I can't do anything to my grandmother's house. She likes it the way it is, she says. Old, ugly, and hot."

"It'll be cool at the North Pole," Dani pointed out bitterly.

Sara looked at her in surprise. Dani was never mad, never. "Hey, Dani, what's wrong?"

Dani rolled off the hammock, grabbed at her light-pen, drew a stroke or two of mane onto the horse on the liquid crystal screen, dropped the pen again, and whirled to face Sara. "Do you know how many steps it takes to cross this room? Five. Five, Sara. That stallion"— she pointed to the holograph to her left—"he wouldn't know what to do if he could only go five steps without bumping into something."

"But you like this room!" Sara protested.

"It's too small. *Everything's* too small. And there are too many people. People everywhere," Dani said, "people nose to nose in the tunnels, people jammed into the monorails, you can't even get a locker to yourself in the rollergym! You should be glad to be going to the North Pole, Sara Green. I'd give anything to be going with you."

Sara stared at her. Suddenly, she smiled. "So, come," she said.

"What?"

"Really. I mean it." Her smile grew. "Grandma wouldn't mind. You could tell her you want to see what one of the last bits of natural Earth looks like. Grandma says that's why she wants Karl and me to come. Tell her you want to see nature and she'll be bound to let you come with us."

"But isn't it awfully expensive to fly to the North Pole?" Dani said doubtfully.

"Grassroots has three puffhovers, and Grandma learned to fly one of them last year. That's how we're going. It is Grassroots business, after all. And why would it be more expensive to fly four of us than three?"

"There probably wouldn't be enough room," Dani said, but her voice was beginning to sound hopeful.

"It's a four-seater."

"Wouldn't Josh just die of jealousy?" Dani said, her eyes starting to sparkle.

"Ask your mom," Sara said decisively. "If she doesn't say no right away, we'll go find Grandma."

✧

"It's like this, Mrs. G.," someone was saying as Sara and Danielle closed the front door behind them on the gasping July heat. "I have a theory about the North Pole. And unless I can actually go there, I'm not going to be able to test it out."

"Joshua!" Danielle said, under her breath. "Wouldn't you just know he'd get to your grandmother first? And there are only four seats on that puffhover!"

"He's not going to go," Sara whispered furiously. "*You* are. And that's that!" But somehow she made herself wait where she was, instead of charging into the room the way she wanted. With those two boys, you needed to plan, not just be mad.

"A North Pole theory, Joshua?"

Grandma's voice sounded interested, and that was a bad sign. It wasn't fair, Sara told herself. The one thing that would have made this trip to the North Pole bearable was having Dani along, and now—

"It has to do with time, Mrs. G. I've been doing quite a few experiments on the subject. You know how all the time zones in the world meet at the North Pole?"

"Umm," Grandma said. "Yes, that's true, they do. Well?"

"So, what time is it there?"

"What time is it at the North Pole?" Grandma repeated thoughtfully.

Think, Sara told herself. But her mind was a blank. Time zones, for heaven's sake! How could she beat those boys at their own game when they'd already got to Grandma with questions like that?

"Well, I don't know, Josh," Grandma went on. "What an unusual question. Maybe time doesn't mean very much up there. There isn't even an ordinary night and day at the Pole, you know. This time of year the sun shines almost the full twenty-four hours. . . ."

Josh waited politely, then helped her out. "Well, if time doesn't mean very much at the North Pole, then either there *is* no real time up there at all, or it's all times at once."

Grandma made that funny little rumble in her throat that meant she was really intrigued. "No time, or all times. Hmm. But people have visited the North Pole over and over again without noticing anything odd about time, Joshua. I mean, they notice the sun, or the lack of it, but—"

"They haven't been thinking about it the way I have," Joshua said very seriously. "That's why I need to go. To check out if my theories are right."

What could she say? Sara thought desperately. What?

"Is this another science project?" Grandma said.

Sara grimaced nervously. Joshua had received country-wide recognition for his last three science projects in a row. He'd already been offered a university scholarship, even though he was only fourteen.

"It might be," Josh said cautiously, "depending on what I find out."

"Then it really is important?" Grandma said.

She's going to let him come, Sara thought. Karl's best friend instead of her own. Sara could hardly bear it. Two of them to put up with!

Karl sensed victory as well. "There *are* four seats in the puffhover, Grandma."

Sara hated her brother at that moment. If Karl hadn't gone straight to Josh the moment he heard they were going to the Arctic, she and Dani would have had time to get in first with Grandma. But oh no. The boys hadn't even asked Joshua's mother for permission first, as she and Dani had done. It wasn't fair!

She stormed down the hall. At the living room door she stopped, glaring at the two boys sitting on the ancient sofa, their legs crossed like grown-ups. "Josh didn't get permission!" she protested.

Her grandmother turned to her. "What's up, Sara?" she asked mildly.

"Dani wants to come to the North Pole, too, Grandma. And *she* got permission to ask you. Oh, Grandma, please, I want Dani to come. It's going to be my birthday. And Dani wants to see nature. Isn't that a better reason to go to the North Pole than a stupid experiment?"

"You're being rude, Sara." Grandma frowned so that her dimple disappeared. "Josh's experiment sounds very interesting." The boys looked smug.

Sara changed tactics quickly. "Okay, but think how much room his stuff will take up in the puffhover. You should just see his place! Clocks everywhere, gears and cogs and wires and bells, and he won't let anybody touch anything, so you have to step over things and around them — and he hasn't even asked his mother if he can come! You always say people should ask their parents."

"Now just a minute — " Karl burst in, rising to his feet.

Sara ignored her brother. Dani had moved up behind her, but Sara knew she wouldn't say anything. Sara would have to do it for her. "Dani wants to see real nature. She told me so, and if you could see her room you'd know it was true—it's all covered with horses in green meadows that're way bigger than five steps wide, and she hates being closed in and she really, really wants to see the North Pole. And I want her to, too!"

She stopped, breathing hard. Joshua was on his feet now.

"I asked first," he said, calmly and reasonably.

"But you didn't ask Mom," Dani put in, surprising Sara a little.

"If she said you could go, she won't say no to me."

"But you—but I—"

"He's my best friend, Grandma."

"Well, *she's* my—"

"Stop, all of you. Stop at once."

Grandma using her Supreme Court justice voice was not to be argued with. Everyone got very quiet. Grandma stepped back a pace or two so that she could take them all in. She was tall and thin, and her hair was pure white, but her clothes were as young as her face: a breathable UV-shirt and pants the exact blue of her eyes. Sara herself was wearing the same style of shirt and pants, she noted resentfully. It was embarrassing that someone that old should dress like a kid. Of course, the only ornament Grandma wore was a wooden brooch carved with the Grassroots logo. Despite her casual clothing, she looked as intimidating as a Greysuit.

"When I first proposed this trip to the Arctic," Grandma said, "neither of you kids wanted to go at all."

"It'd be different if Dani—"

"If Josh came—"

Grandma ignored their outbursts. "What I offered you two was an opportunity. This world has only a few pock-

15

ets of real life left. You take it as normal, because it is all you know. But it's not normal, it is not acceptable, and I wanted you to know it. No, be quiet, I'm not finished. *I* couldn't convince you two about the advantages of visiting the Arctic, but apparently your friends could. For that reason alone they deserve to come."

"*Both* of them?"

"I can come, Mrs. G? Really?"

"There'll be room for my equipment, won't there?"

"But the puffhover's only got four seats!"

"Four passenger seats," Grandma said coolly. "You've forgotten that I'll be flying the thing. And there's always room for the pilot!"

Chapter Two

"TAKE a good look," Gwyneth Green said to the four children. "You've only got a little while to see Ottawa from the air before I key in the turbojet." She was seated in the pilot's central swivel, surrounded by instruments. The children were in a semicircle around her, strapped into the thickly padded seats of the puffhover with their backs to the outside wall.

In the short time they had been in the air Danielle had got used to the soft, repetitive poof made by the rotating hoverpads, and the dizzying feeling that the transparent floor beneath them wasn't really there at all. She didn't need Mrs. G's suggestion to take a good look at the city below them; she was already leaning forward as far as her straps would let her. But Sara—Dani took a quick glance to her left and frowned—Sara was sitting far back in her seat, looking straight ahead.

"What's the matter, Sara?" Dani whispered.

"Nothing."

"Why aren't you looking?"

"Don't want to."

Karl pointed. "There's Parliament Hill," he said. "Look how green it is!"

"Paint," his grandmother replied. "They paved it over when it got too difficult to keep the grass alive."

"Hey, look at the Parliament Buildings!" Karl added excitedly. Dani could see that he wasn't listening to his grandmother at all.

Joshua had a stopwatch in his lap and was frowning down at his wrist computer. Now and then he used his light-pen to scribble something on the tiny screen. "I wonder what going turbo will do?" he muttered. He raised his voice without changing position. "Mrs. G, what's our exact speed in turbo?"

"I have no idea, Josh. Not light speed, but fast."

"There's the trillium flag on the House of Commons." Karl again. Danielle wanted to smile, superior Karl sounding so excited.

"The wind really makes it fly, doesn't it?" he went on, not noticing that Joshua wasn't paying attention. "Flags should always be outside."

"*People* should be outside," his grandmother said.

The bitter note in her voice caught everyone's attention. "We go outside, Grandma," Karl said.

"Only when you can't find a climate-controlled tunnel or a monorail or a puffhover to take you where you need to go," Mrs. Green replied.

"Puffhovers aren't so awful," Joshua put in politely. "Solar and atomic power don't pollute. And in a puffhover you can go places you couldn't get to otherwise. Like the North Pole."

Mrs. G laughed. "And that puts *me* in my place, thank you very much. All right, Josh, I agree with you about puffhovers. I wouldn't have learned to fly one if I didn't."

The puffhover was an odd craft, disk-shaped except for its pointed nose, which was designed to cut wind resistance. The small waste-conversion booth was in the narrowed front, with a spigot for drinking water and a tiny microwave oven. The rear of the puffhover was slung with hammocks. Each of the children had been allowed to take one softpack, and Josh had one extra small sack of equipment for his experiment. These, along with Mrs. G's softpack, were securely tied into one hammock. The second hammock was full of dehydrated food, the third was jammed with bedrolls, and the fourth contained technical equipment and the standard northern zipsuits that they would all wear over their ordinary clothes after they reached the Arctic.

The hammocks would serve as beds for the four children once they were unpacked. Mrs. G would sleep in the pilot's swivel, which she had shown them could be made to lie flat if you took out a section of the instrument panel. They would cook, eat, and sleep aboard the puffhover, but it was obvious that there would be little room for any other activities. That was, Mrs. G had said, what the outside was for.

An adult of average height could just stand upright in the center of the craft. Mrs. G had had to stoop. Today she was wearing an ancient pair of faded blue pants that she called jeans, with a buttoned jacket in a matching fabric, a pair of mock-leather gloves and scuffed lace-up boots. Danielle knew Sara was embarrassed about her grandmother's old-fashioned clothes, but she herself liked them. They looked as if they were meant for big spaces.

Mrs. G had her attention on the naviscreen in front of her, and so it was Joshua, now that he had stopped looking at his computer long enough to take in the view, who pointed out the seamless blue-green roofs on the Parliament Buildings. "They look just like old copper, don't they?" he asked cheerfully.

"That's what they are, Josh," Sara said. "We took it in history."

"They used to be," Josh demurred, "but now they're plastique. The copper ones were ruined by acid rain."

"Kids Sara's age don't have a clue about acid rain, Josh," Karl said loftily.

"Sara does," Dani said loyally. "We both do."

"Okay, then, what is it?"

Dani looked at Sara, who was silent. She cleared her throat. "Well—uh—it's a kind of rain. Kind of—acid."

"Wow, Josh," Karl said, grinning. "I didn't know your sister was so smart. Acid rain is rain that's acid. Wow."

"Shut up, Karl," Sara said angrily. "Why don't you tell us what it is, since you're so smart?"

It was Josh who answered, his voice absentminded as he peered at his computer. "In the olden days rain got contaminated with the by-products of the burning of fossil fuels. People made laws against it in North America and Europe, but too late to save a lot of things. Trees, those roofs. . . . Hey, Mrs. G, will you warn me before we go turbo? I want to use my stopwatch."

She nodded. They flew on in silence. Airspeed restrictions over the city kept the puffhover to a cruising speed that gave them a good view. Ottawa was like a toy model of a city, with almost every building concrete and square. Only the Parliament Buildings and a few private houses stood separately, slate roofs baking in the heat, chimneys carefully capped. The Ottawa River was sluggish and brown and reflected no light at all, despite the relentless sun overhead. Dani could see ant-size robots in the spotted green ditch that had once been the Rideau Canal.

"Agrifertil experiment," Joshua said. There were a few patches of shrubbery where the robots were. They looked cool and inviting.

Karl unbuckled himself and went over to Mrs. G's side. She said calmly, "In three minutes we're going turbo, Karl. You'll be plastered all over that floor if you aren't in your seat when it happens."

Karl nodded, but he stayed. "I'm going to learn to fly the moment I turn fifteen," he said. "The best jobs go to the people who know the most things."

"The best jobs go to the people who aren't lazy like you," Sara jeered.

"Hey, brat, *you're* the expert in our family on how to spend hours doing nothing."

Mrs. G frowned at them, her blue eyes annoyed. "Enough, Karl. You, too, Sara. This is supposed to be fun, not a battlefield."

Dani didn't like Karl's superior ways any more than Sara did, but to accuse Karl of being lazy was just plain wrong. Karl was on the school council as well as almost every sports team, and he had to study hard every night to get the good grades Josh tossed off so easily. Sara and Karl were always bickering, but today Sara's voice was higher than usual, and her lips looked like two thin lines. What was bothering her?

Mrs. G pointed. "See that green patch down there?" They all looked, all but Sara. "That's the famous Verdant Meadows. It's under a dome, of course. Only the Greysuits get to enjoy it."

Danielle had never seen so many trees. It was like looking down on a blurry green carpet, except for the breaks where the mansions were. Was this what a forest was like? "It's beautiful," she said softly.

"Beeches, maples, even one willow," Mrs. G said, nodding. "The willow took some doing. They need so much water."

She keyed in some instructions to the autopilot. "Time to go back to your seat, Karl," Mrs. G said. "Ten seconds. I mean it."

He didn't exactly run, Dani noticed, but he didn't saunter, either. She grinned at Sara, who didn't seem to see, her fingers holding the arm rests in a white-knuckled grip. She's scared, Dani thought suddenly. But no, that didn't make sense. It was always Sara who was first in the rollergym to try the impossible stunts, always Sara who suggested the tricks they played on Josh and Karl, always Sara who roared down halls at school while Dani, her quieter friend, tried to keep up.

Mrs. G's fingers flew over the keyboard. "Ready, Josh?" He nodded, index finger poised over his stopwatch. "Three. Two. One. Now."

There was a sudden feeling of pressure in Dani's chest, a billowing puff in her ears. The chair she sat in seemed to be turning to elastic. Her body went with it, strangely shapeless, stretched. Someone was struggling to say something, but it was too hard to decipher the words. Dani kept her eyes closed. Colors streamed behind her lids, bright sunny colors, glitter. It seemed that a long time passed.

"There," Mrs. G. said. It was her normal tone. Dani could hear her perfectly.

She opened her eyes. The light in the puffhover was different. Softer, somehow. Cooler.

"Now *there's* something to see," said Mrs. G, pointing down at the floor window. "The Great Boreal Forest. We're still a long way south of the Arctic, but I took us out of turbo so you could see it. Few people do, nowadays."

"It's huge," Joshua murmured, almost in awe, leaning forward as far as he could.

"Pretty good," Karl agreed.

Dani said nothing. She couldn't. Down below her was wet earth and growing things and green, so much green. There was blue, too, clear lakes of glittering water, rivers, waterfalls. She stared and stared, and her chest, so tight only a few minutes before, felt as big as the forest below her, wide open and full of a kind of air she'd never known before, fresh, cool, and free. It was her imagination, she

22

told herself; she was breathing the climate-controlled air of the puffhover; she couldn't be feeling that coolness inside her lungs, or smelling that tart, alive scent that the televids described and she'd tried so often to imagine. For some reason her eyes felt prickly.

"You're not looking, Sara," Mrs. Green said.

"I did. I saw it."

"Sara?"

"I *saw* it, I said!"

Mrs. G shrugged. After a moment she turned to the others. "Maple and beech, hawthorn and willow and cottonwood. None of them are in the south anymore. We have to make sure they don't disappear from here, too."

For some time no one said anything. Then Mrs. G shook herself. "Time to go on. Can't let those Greysuits think they've got the Arctic to themselves." Her fingers flew over the keyboard again. "Ready?" she called. "Turbo — *now!*"

✧

They landed blind, coming out of turbo only to find that Mrs. G had programmed the whole procedure, including closing the viewing window. For the few moments of their descent there was nothing to see, and they wouldn't have known they were descending at all had it not been for the whine of the hoverpads. There was no bump on landing, but the whirring hoverpads slowed and finally stopped altogether. The puffhover settled into silence with the tiniest of sighs.

"Are we at the Pole?" Karl asked.

Mrs. G unlatched the instrument panel, got out of her chair, and, stooping a little, stretched her arms wide. "Not yet," she said. "Adam Duguay, my particular Greysuit, isn't going to be at the Pole until tomorrow. We're going to camp here until tomorrow morning, and fly the rest of the way then. It won't take long."

Joshua looked pleased. "Will I be able to do some experiments here?" he asked, eyeing his sack of equipment in the hammock at the rear.

"As long as you do them outside," Mrs. G said. "We all need fresh air and exercise. Unpack what you need. And we'd better get into our zipsuits."

"Where are we, exactly?" Dani asked.

"Ellesmere Island," Mrs. G said. She sounds happy, Dani thought. "The most northerly part of Ellesmere Island, at that. I'd be willing to bet this is the farthest north any of us will ever be and still be on dry land."

"I'm dying to get out," Dani said.

Mrs. G laughed. "Good for you, Dani."

"I'm not feeling very well," Sara said suddenly.

Mrs. G had been loosening the tie-down clamps on the bottom hammock. She turned at this. "What's the matter, dear?" she asked.

"I just don't feel well."

"Headache?" Sara nodded. "Sick to your stomach?" Again Sara nodded.

Mrs. G hurried to her side. "Let's see your throat."

Obediently Sara opened her mouth. Mrs. G took a tiny laser light from her belt and shone it inside. "Nothing obvious," Mrs. G said. She felt Sara's forehead. "No fever, either."

"Maybe I'm allergic."

"To what?"

"This place. The air must be full of horrible things."

"We haven't opened the outside vents," Mrs. G said.

"Well, *I* don't know," Sara said querulously. "I feel terrible, that's all. Can't I stay on board the puffhover and sleep while the rest of you go out?"

Mrs. G pursed her lips at her granddaughter. "You don't want to go with us?" Sara shook her head. "I see." She dragged the last word out. Sara shifted uncomfortably.

Dani looked from one of them to the other. Mrs. G had a funny look in her eyes, almost as if she didn't believe that Sara was telling the truth. "She does look white, Mrs. G," Dani said loyally. Sara sent her a grateful glance.

"She always looks white, Danielle," Mrs. G said. "You all look white. It's one of the reasons why I want you to go outside for a change. You need some sun."

She turned in a businesslike way and went back to the hammocks.

"The sun causes cancer," Sara said loudly to her grandmother's back. "There's a hole in the ozone layer, remember? It isn't like when you were our age, Grandma. Nothing's like when you were our age!"

"You know that the Ottawa water supply has been fortified with long-lasting antioxidants," Mrs. G said, speaking firmly, but not facing her granddaughter. "None of you will get cancer from going out in the sun."

Equally firmly Sara said, "Well, I can't take the heat. Not when I'm feeling so rotten."

"It isn't hot up here in the north the way it is in Ottawa," Josh put in helpfully.

"You keep out of this!" Sara hissed at him.

Mrs. G turned. "Be quiet, Sara. Josh is right. Do you all know which zipsuit fits you?"

Sara threw off her straps and jumped to her feet. "Don't you hear me, Grandma? I don't *feel* well! It's my birthday tomorrow, in case you've forgotten—"

"Who could forget it?" Karl muttered. "You remind us every five minutes."

25

"—and if I go outside now, I might be too sick to enjoy it!"

Dani went to her friend's side and put her arm around her. She couldn't say anything. Sara must be really sick to behave like this.

"I haven't forgotten your birthday, Sara," Mrs. G said, very calmly. "But that's not what we're talking about. *Especially* because you're not feeling well, you should get some fresh air and exercise. It'll make you feel better."

"What if I throw up? Or pass out?" she asked threateningly.

"We'll cross that bridge when we come to it. *If* we come to it."

Under Dani's arm, Sara's body went rigid. "You don't believe me, do you?" Sara demanded, her face contorted. "You don't think I'm sick at all."

Mrs. G's blue eyes showed concern, but her voice was steady. "I don't know what to think. You are behaving rather immaturely. Perhaps it is because you're sick, as you say. Perhaps, however—well, maybe you're just a little bit afraid."

Dani felt her friend shudder. She hugged her even tighter. "Afraid? What would I be afraid of?"

"A lot of people nowadays are afraid of going outside, Sara," Mrs. G said, suddenly gentle. "It's called agoraphobia, the fear of open spaces. The way people live nowadays, it's not surprising that so many people have adapted to crowded conditions by learning to fear the opposite. If you *were* afraid, you wouldn't be alone."

"I'm not afraid!" Sara said loudly. "I'm not feeling well, that's all. But since nobody but Dani seems to care about that . . ." She stared challengingly around the puffhover, her green eyes blazing in her white face, then marched to her grandmother's side. "Where's my

26

zipsuit?" she demanded, plowing through the piles on one of the hammocks. "Or I'll go out without one if you like. I'll go swimming in the ocean, too. It's bound to be polluted, but I don't care. I'm not afraid. You'll see."

"You'll wear your zipsuit," her grandmother said calmly, "and you won't go swimming at all. It's one thing to be brave, but stupid is something else altogether."

Chapter Three

S ARA pressed her back to the far wall of the puffhover, her eyes white rimmed as Grandma opened the sliding doors to the outside. Her moment of defiance had passed. Dressed for the Arctic, she watched almost in a panic as light flooded into the puffhover, wild and cool and brilliant, not at all like the smoggy glare of Ottawa or the controlled overhead panel lights of the puffhover. What's wrong with me? she thought, her hands clenched. Why can't I be like Grandma, standing so casually in the doorway, looking outside?

Outside.

An uncontrollable tremor shook her entire body. I am getting a fever, she told herself. I am, no matter what Grandma says.

She wished her mother were there. Mom knew about germs and things. She wouldn't just touch Sara's forehead or look down her throat and say she wasn't sick. She'd use a proper thermometer and take a swab and then she'd send her right to bed until the results of the swab came. Mom was pretty casual about most things, but never germs. She wouldn't dream of allowing Sara to go outside when she felt so terrible.

Under the sun visor of her zipsuit her face was bare. She wished the zipsuit came with a face cover. A huge nothingness waited out there, and she had to enter it with her face exposed. Grandma could say what she liked, they would all probably get cancer. I'm going to throw up, Sara told herself. For a brief, savage moment she hoped she would make a real mess.

She looked at Josh and Karl, kidding each other about who looked more like a spaceman; at Danielle standing quietly, hugging herself to contain her excitement. Nobody else seemed to be wanting to throw up at the thought of being outside in that empty expanse. Why was she, Sara, the only one?

Grandma pressed a button, and the narrow portastairs descended. She followed them down. Her voice floated up to the four children. "It's a lovely, sunny day. Not even a mosquito cloud on the horizon. We hardly need these zipsuits."

No buildings, Sara thought. No people. Just one big emptiness. She hadn't let herself imagine it properly until they'd begun this journey. But then she'd looked through that glass floor showing her the enormity of the world outside. And that forest . . . She shivered again. In Ottawa she was in control, capable. She knew where everything important was; she knew what to expect. Not here.

It made it worse that she felt so sick. How could any-body be in control of anything, feeling dizzy and faint and nobody believing her? I could be dying, she told herself bitterly, and they'd still make me go out there.

"Listen, Sara," Karl said, coming over to where she still stood, her back glued to the puffhover's rear wall. "If you're really sick—"

"Why is it so hard for people to believe it?" she demanded angrily. "Just because *you* feel great doesn't mean everyone in the world has to. Why don't you just leave me alone?"

He stared at her, then nodded abruptly. "Fine. So if you're coming, you'd better do it now, and you'd better go first. No one wants to be underneath you on the stairs if you decide to faint."

"Sara never faints," Dani said, her color bright. "You go first, Karl, or maybe it's *you* who's too nervous?" She rarely stood up to Karl, who was the biggest of the four of them, and the quickest tempered.

"Me, nervous? Don't be dumb."

"Prove it."

"Oh, stuff it, you two," Josh said impatiently. He had his sack in one gloved hand and was tugging at Karl with the other. "I want to get my equipment set up. You said you'd help with the measurements, Karl. It'll take two of us to pace things out." Karl gave Dani one last angry look and followed Josh to the door of the puffhover.

Still Sara stood unmoving. Dani came over to her. "I'll hold your arm," she said very quietly.

"Sara, Dani," Grandma called, poking her head back in the puffhover at them. "I can't shut this thing up until you two are both out."

There was no way around it. "All right," Sara said. "All right."

Again Grandma disappeared below. Sara made herself cross the floor of the puffhover. At least it wasn't transparent any longer. Dani's hand on her arm felt good. Sara swallowed determinedly. She wouldn't throw up. Not on Dani. The brightness ahead of her was giving her a headache. She closed her eyes and let Dani guide her.

They were at the open door of the puffhover now. "I love it," Dani said. "Oh, Sara, look at it."

Slowly Sara opened her eyes, squinting into the Arctic afternoon.

They were on dry land, more or less, though there seemed to be as many ponds as there were grayish green knolls and bare, flat rocks. There was water almost every-where, for the puffhover had set down on a jagged

31

narrow peninsula cut by fiords. The encroaching sea was very clear and pale and looked to Sara to be terribly cold, but she could see a big green patch in it, too, just off-shore by the puffhover. Somehow that green was easier to look at than anything else, so she rested her eyes on it.

"Grass," Danielle whispered in awe, seeing the direction of her gaze. "Grass, growing in the water."

It did look like that, wavy green spears like the old-fashioned meadow grasses in Dani's holograph of the stallion.

"It must be a kind of seaweed," Sara said, and was pleased how steadily she got it out.

"That's right," her grandmother's voice said. "It's seaweed. Eelgrass, actually. Good for you, Sara."

Sara shifted her gaze from that patch of green to where Grandma waited patiently at the foot of the stairs. With her white hair covered by the hood of the zipsuit and that ridiculous jean jacket poking its collar out under her chin, Grandma looked young and strange, someone else altogether than the opinionated ex–chief justice who made Greysuits tremble. She smiled up at Sara then, a startlingly understanding smile. I know, that smile seemed to say; it's all right, I'll look after you. Sara tried to be angry again, tried to remember how mean Grandma was being, making her come out here when she felt so sick. But that smile made it hard.

"Eelgrass is very important to the birds and sea creatures," Grandma went on calmly. "Come down, and we'll take a closer look. I'll bet we'll see some fish. You come down first, Sara, and then Dani. There isn't room on the stairs for the two of you side by side."

Grandma was holding one of her hands out toward her. Dani was right behind her. Sara began to descend.

I'm sick, she told herself. I'm only scared because I'm sick.

"I didn't think anything grew in the Arctic," Dani said behind her.

Sara didn't say anything. She was concentrating on getting down the stairs. But Grandma replied, "Even when I was young, Dani, Arctic summers were apparently quite gentle. I never got up here to see for myself, I'm sorry to say. But these days, with so much of the ice cap melting, it's even more temperate. A lot of plants grow here even in winter. Good, Sara, you're down. That's it, hold my arm. Dani, you take her other one. I'm just going to close up the puffhover" — she keyed in a sequence to the autolock, and the doors above their heads slid shut — "and then we'll go look at that eelgrass."

They passed Karl and Josh, doing something with a tape measure and a stopwatch. They got as near to the patch of eelgrass as they could, though it was farther offshore than it had seemed from the puffhover. Still, Dani swore she could see fish swimming in and out of the wavy green fronds. Sara looked longingly over her shoulder at the puffhover, but neither Grandma nor Dani seemed ready to go back. "Let's head toward that big boulder," Grandma said after a few minutes.

It was an obvious landmark, a single jutting stone sticking out of the empty landscape quite a long way from the puffhover. Sara breathed deeply. She nodded.

It did feel good to stretch her legs, she told herself. She tried to concentrate on that, on what she was inside herself, contained and controlled. She tried not to notice all that empty space outside. But a mild wind was blowing, just enough to stir a long red curl of her hair that had somehow escaped the headgear of the zipsuit.

That breath of wind moving her hair, like fingers she didn't know stroking her, drew her outside her own self-absorption, so that she had to notice where she was and what she was doing. If it hadn't been for her grandmother's firm hold on her arm, Sara didn't know what she would have done. Grandma's voice helped, too. She talked the whole time, pointing out the grey-and-black lichens growing on the flat rock tables, and the startling orange ones covering the jutting boulder that was their destination.

"Orange lichens survive only in pollution-free atmospheres," Grandma was saying. "Even then, they need a fair bit of bird dung to grow. I'll bet that big boulder's a common perch for a snowy owl or a hawk." She kept talking, almost as if she knew how important it was to Sara. "There might even be loons here. You know, the bird that used to be on the Canadian dollar coin? I loved them when I was growing up. You haven't lived until you've heard a loon call on a moonlit lake."

Sara listened. She wouldn't throw up as long as Grandma kept talking.

"Willows," Grandma said, pointing to a flat area of twining branches covered in green leaves. They weren't even as high as a bush, the stems pressed almost flat to the ground. There were flowers, too, yellow and purple tussocks: tiny, but with a surprising, delicate beauty. "Arctic poppy," Grandma said, pointing, "moss pink, saxifrage, vetch." Sara let herself look. It was like a rock garden she had seen once in a televid. Only instead of being tiny and contained, it was the whole huge Arctic.

The whole Arctic. She shuddered, the sickness returning. She moved closer to Grandma.

"Time to go back now," Grandma said at once.

"Already?" Dani asked in disappointment. "We haven't got to the boulder yet. And it's only five o'clock."

"I know that, dear. But there's supper to make, and I have comp work to do before I can meet Adam Duguay tomorrow. You can go out later on by yourself if you want."

"Or maybe Sara and I can go together," Dani said hopefully.

Sara turned her face away. She couldn't come out here again. She just couldn't. Dani would have to understand that. She would, of course. She always understood the things that mattered to Sara. It was one of the reasons Sara liked her so much.

✧

Dani stood at the open door of the puffhover, staring out over the tundra to the splashes of neon purple that were Josh and Karl in their zipsuits. They were certainly too far away to hear a call for supper. Somebody was going to have to go and tell them. "All those watches and clocks," Dani joked to Sara, "and they haven't noticed it's nearly six."

"This casserole cooks on the lowest power," Sara said, opening the microwave and stirring briskly. "It won't be ready for half an hour, at least. But still . . . Are the boys really far?"

"Yes," Dani said. "I'd better go get them. Okay with you, Mrs. G?"

"Mmm," Mrs. G said, clicking through computer screens.

"Do you want to come, too, Sara?"

Sara shook her head, her back to Dani. "Got to watch that this thing doesn't dry out," she said, punching buttons on the microwave.

Her voice was cheerful enough. As soon as they had got back on board the puffhover, Sara had returned to her normal self. She had even volunteered to cook supper. That was funny, if she had been sick to her stomach all afternoon, Dani thought. Had she really been sick? Or was Mrs. G right, and was Sara just afraid of the outside? The possibility shook Dani. Sara, afraid! How could she be, when Dani wasn't?

Dani loved it here. She loved the freshness of the air, and the quiet. She loved the iron-grey water, and the patches of green in it; she loved the white moss, soft as sponges; the low, leafy scrub. She especially loved the flowers. They were tiny but perfect, dotting the dull grey-green tundra with their splashes of color.

Dani bounded off the portastairs, hurrying until she reached the first clump of purple vetch, then bending to examine it. The curling green stems seemed to grab her finger when she touched them. She looked up. What a sky!—so wide, so empty. She might almost have had the world to herself. Of course the boys were out here, too, but quite far away, really, and their backs were to Dani. If she didn't deliberately look at them, she could pretend they weren't here at all.

She aimed for the boulder speckled with orange lichen, keeping it between her and the boys. Now and then she bent over to smell flowers, or stretched tall to sweep the sky for birds. It would be fun to see hawks—or maybe loons. *You haven't lived until you've heard a loon call on a moonlit lake.* Loons must be very special birds to make Mrs. G talk about them like that. Dani wished she'd asked her what they looked like.

The boys were on the other side of the big rock, not too far away now. They hadn't noticed her coming. She could call them from here, but she didn't feel like it. She wanted to hug the feeling of having the Arctic to herself for a while longer. There was still time—Sara had said half an hour. . . . She sat down, her back to the boulder and her knees to her chest, and squinted into the clear sky. A bird might come if she kept still enough.

After a minute she heard the boys talking. Their voices grew louder. Approaching the boulder, Dani guessed. She listened.

". . . nothing all afternoon but lay out the tape measure and set chronometers and write down the times you call out to me," Karl was complaining. "I wish you'd tell me what all this stuff is for."

Dani, too, wanted to hear what it was for. Josh was so secretive about everything. He hadn't even told his best friend what he was trying to find out.

Joshua muttered something Dani couldn't hear.

"Hey, I'm not asking for the password to your computer," Karl said, "just a little ordinary information."

"You'll think I'm crazy," Josh said.

"You? Come on."

"It sounds crazy," Josh said. "Even to me, sometimes. But I've been thinking about it and thinking about it, and I just can't help wondering—" He broke off.

"Give," Karl said.

"It's nothing to do with our measurements today. What we've been doing here is interesting, and the data will be useful someday, but as far as these clocks are concerned, it's all just a smoke screen."

Dani's ears pricked up. She pushed herself hard against the boulder, praying that the boys would stay on the other side of it long enough for her to hear everything.

"A *smoke screen?*" Karl demanded. "You mean I've been walking my feet off just for show?"

"Only part of it was just for show. The clock part. See, Karl, it might not work. My theory, I mean. I didn't want to mention it until I'd tested it, not even to you."

37

"What theory? And what about those clocks?"

"It's something that I don't think anyone else has thought of. You know I don't like to predict things without testing them first. That's why—"

"The clocks, Josh," Karl said impatiently.

"Give me a chance! I'll tell you. But remember, it's only a theory. And for heaven's sake, keep it to yourself. Those girls would be all over us if they knew." His voice lowered so that Dani had to strain to hear. "You know what I said to Mrs. G about what time it might be at the North Pole? Well—"

"Well what?"

"Well—" Again Josh broke off. Dani didn't think she had ever heard her brother sound so unsure of himself.

"For heaven's sake!" Karl said exasperatedly.

"All right. All right! Well, because all the time zones in the world meet at the North Pole, it might actually be possible to—well, all times might coexist there."

"I don't—"

"Periods of history might sort of—well, overlap. Kind of like—well, like having all times available to you, if you wanted them. I think"—Joshua's voice went lower still, and suddenly faster—"this is the crazy part, Karl, but I can't help but wonder if the North Pole might be a place where you could travel through time, if you knew how."

Dani's eyes widened, and she hugged her knees even more tightly to her chest. Time travel! And Josh wasn't kidding. She could tell by his voice.

"Like in a time machine?" Karl demanded, his voice incredulous. "That *is* crazy, Josh. I mean, hey, I know you get the best grades in science every year, but that really is—"

"I know," Josh said grimly. "That's exactly why I didn't tell you before. I knew you wouldn't believe me unless the evidence was right in front of your eyes."

"People have been visiting the North Pole for years and years, Josh, and nobody's ever gone to another time. How can the North Pole be a time machine if nobody's ever used it?"

"Even a time machine would have to be turned on. If people didn't know how to turn it on, they wouldn't go anywhere."

"But time travel!"

Josh made a frustrated sound. "Look, why don't we just forget the whole thing. I never said it would happen for sure. I only said it might. But if you can't believe that there's even a possibility—"

"It's really far out."

"I said forget it!"

"I can't. If you're right, the thing's fabulous. And hey, buddy, it's not like your ideas are usually wrong."

Karl had a point, Dani thought. If it had been anybody else who'd come up with the idea of time traveling . . . But it wasn't anybody else. It was Joshua—the same Joshua who had invented a way of biodegrading color-bonded plastic for a science project at school. He'd got first prize in all of Ontario for that one, and now he had a patent pending.

Karl was silent for a moment or two, thinking. When he spoke again his voice was different. "The North Pole, a time machine . . . If you're right—"

"I don't know that I am. It's just a possibility, that's all. And I want to test it. Anyway, I don't think the North Pole could be a machine. No on-off switches, nothing like that. What I kind of imagine is"—his voice went a little higher pitched—"well, maybe I see it as an invisible doorway, or a bunch of doorways all together. Walk through one, and you might be in the ancient past. Dinosaurs, Karl."

"Or maybe we'd end up in France, fighting alongside the Three Musketeers," Karl put in eagerly.

"Or maybe watching Edison making that light bulb glow for forty hours. . . ."

Dani could tell how excited her brother was. That, more than anything, impressed her. Josh really believed in the possibility of what he was saying. For the first time she let herself imagine it. Time travel! Of course it couldn't be, but — if it could . . . The past in front of your eyes, just by walking through a doorway . . .

"The thing is," Josh said, "if even one time door does exist, it's got to be locked. Otherwise everybody who goes to the North Pole would go through it automatically. And we know that doesn't happen. We'd need some kind of key to open it."

"Oh." Disappointed. "How do you unlock an invisible door?"

"I've been trying to think. Suppose the key was an object from the past. That might take us to the time the object first existed. But everybody goes to the North Pole with things that were made in the past. So it would have to be an object that's somehow logically connected with time."

"Your chronometers!" Karl hissed out the word. "One of your old clocks! *That's* what you brought them for!"

"Yes." Josh added quickly, "I don't *know,* though, remember. I'm just guessing. And even if one of them might work as the key, we'd still have to figure out how to use it that way."

"A clock does make sense," Karl said. He laughed happily. "Hey, can't you just see it? You and me, traveling through time!"

"People won't want us to, of course, not on our own. That's why—"

Karl laughed again. "Now I understand all that business with clocks today! So that when we want to do things with the clocks at the North Pole, Grandma won't even ask why."

"Mrs. G is okay," Josh said cautiously, "but she isn't a *scientist*, is she? And old people always want to protect you."

"So when we get to the Pole, we try out one clock after another. . . . How, exactly?"

"I don't know. Wind them. Let them run down. Stop the hands. Break them off. I don't know. We'll have to experiment to see what works. Maybe nothing will. I told you, Karl, I don't *know* time travel is possible."

"Time travel." Karl's voice was awed, suddenly.

"If it works."

"Just you and me, Josh? No one else. Not the brats."

"If it works," Josh said again.

There was a long silence.

Not the brats, Dani thought.

"I suppose we can stop taking measurements, now," Josh said. "I've got a lot of data."

"For next year's science project, huh?" Karl laughed again. "Okay. I'll reel the tape measure back in."

"No. We'll have to go back for it. I fixed the other end with a rock, remember?"

They stopped talking then. Dani waited for a little while longer and then got to her feet. Her heart pounded with a combination of excitement and anger. It wasn't that she believed in time travel. Even if it was Josh who'd come up with the idea, Josh who was ten times as smart as anybody else . . . Well, that wasn't the point. The point was that those two had decided that if they *did* figure out how to do it, they weren't going to take her and Sara with them. It was mean and rotten of them, even more mean and rotten than usual. Of course they wouldn't go into the past. But if they did . . . She wanted to run back right away to the puffhover and tell Sara what she had heard, but she still had her errand to do.

She rounded the boulder. The boys were a little way off, their backs to her. "Josh!" she shouted, making herself pant as if she'd been running to catch up to them.

The boys turned. "What do *you* want, tweenie brain?"

"Supper's ready," Dani called, her color flaring. Tweenie brain! She didn't wait while they went to pick up their equipment, but turned and ran for the puffhover. She had to see Sara. Sara would have a plan for this when she heard. Sara could always be counted on to have a plan.

Chapter Four

DANIELLE had never before realized just how small one puffhover could be. There was nowhere in it for her to be alone with Sara. The only private place in the entire craft was the waste-conversion unit, and it wasn't big enough to hold two people. What Joshua was planning made too long a story, with the boys' voices already audible outside the puffhover.

Dani managed to hiss a quick, "Got something important to tell you. Outside, after supper?" into Sara's ear while she stood at the microwave, frowning into the tofu-carrot casserole.

"Outside?" Sara repeated dumbly.

It was only then, seeing Sara's face, that Dani knew how difficult it was going to be.

Gloomily Dani wandered to her chair, watching as the boys clumped up the portastairs and swaggered inside. Their faces were full of their secret. They'd be grinning at each other all night in that lofty way they had and calling her and Sara "tweenies" and "brats" and thinking they had put something over on them. Well, they hadn't. She knew what they were up to. The trouble was, she didn't know how to use what she knew. It was always Sara, not Dani, who figured out exactly what to do when the boys got especially obnoxious, always Sara who made the plans.

The doors to the puffhover slid shut behind the boys. Only then did Sara turn to them. "You're late," she grumbled. "I'm going to have to reheat everything."

"They were a long way away, dear," Mrs. G reminded her. "Did you get all the data you need, Josh?" She put down her light-pen, stretched, and smiled.

"Most of it," Josh said. "I'll need to be right at the Pole for the rest." Dani wanted to glare at him, but restrained herself.

"Sara's been working hard," Mrs. G said. "It really smells good in here, dear."

"Thanks, Grandma."

"Anything smells good if you're hungry," Karl said.

Mrs. G made an exasperated face at him. "Couldn't you even try, Karl? One little compliment to your sister wouldn't kill you."

"If it didn't, her cooking probably would."

"Karl!"

"Never mind, Grandma," Sara said airily. "Eat it or wear it, I always say. I think Karl would look good in a tofu toga, don't you?" She dumped the casserole back in the microwave and jabbed the buttons on.

Karl shut up. Dani wished she could handle Josh the way Sara did Karl. But Josh was smarter than Karl, and Dani knew she wasn't quick, the way Sara was. It always took her ages to think of the right thing to say, and by then the time to say it was long gone.

It was the same with having ideas. She had them sometimes, but always too late. When she was really little, before she knew Sara, other children would be slopping around, bored, wanting something to do, and Dani would think and think, but by the time she finally got an idea the other kids would already be off somewhere, playing something without her. Sometimes she would save up her ideas for the next time, but she soon learned that what she came up with usually made other children laugh. Once in free-movement class at school she had

44

suggested that they put on a mime play about horses, and she would never forget the laughter and the blank looks the rest of the children sent her way.

Sara hadn't been in her school then, of course. Sara would never have laughed. Sara would have agreed to do it, and they would have started, and then somehow the horses grazing on their open meadow would have turned into robbers running down a pitch-black tunnel or space-women exploring the undermines of Xanth, and it would have been so much fun that even Dani would have forgotten how it was all supposed to go in the first place.

"Anybody besides me feel like eating outside?" Mrs. G asked.

Dani held her breath. Maybe if the boys did, she and Sara could have a private talk over dinner.

"Not me," Josh said.

Karl agreed. "Nowhere to sit down out there."

"Then I guess I'll stay in, too," Mrs. G said. "But it seems a terrible waste of all that beautiful fresh air." She caught sight of Dani's disappointed face. "But if you want to, Dani, I'll—"

"No," Dani said quickly, "no, it's all right. Maybe I'll go out again later." She looked meaningfully at Sara, who was serving out the casserole.

Just for a moment, Sara looked back, her shoulders stiff, her back stubborn. Dani knew what that meant. Sara understood very well that Dani had something private to tell her, but she wasn't going to let her tell it, not if it meant going outside. Sara, who was never afraid of anything, must have been really afraid today.

Poor Sara, Dani thought. The one girl in school all the kids looked up to, the point leader at the rollergym, always the first to try hard things like bungee jumping and swimming against bigger kids. How she must hate

45

the idea that she had been scared to do something as seemingly easy as going outside!

Except that she wouldn't believe she *had* been scared. She had gotten sick rather than believe it this afternoon. What would she do now that Dani needed her to go outside again?

"You're only serving out four plates, Sara," Mrs. G said. "Karl was only joking."

"I know, Grandma," Sara said, her voice quivering a little, "but I don't want anything to eat. I'm feeling sick again."

"You really don't look well," Mrs. G said in concern. She got up at once, then put an arm around Sara and led her to a chair. "Oh dear. When you were sick earlier, I thought—and then I made you come outside with us! No wonder you were so shaky."

Poor Mrs. G, Dani thought.

"Is it your stomach?" Sara's grandmother went on. "Are you going to throw up?"

"I don't know. It comes and goes. Sometimes I feel fine, and then it hits again and all I want to do is lie down and sleep."

"I'll clear off your hammock." Mrs. G hurried and emptied the second one from the bottom. "Now, dear, you go to bed. We'll try not to disturb you."

Sara moved slowly to the hammock. Dani couldn't be angry with her friend. Sara wasn't consciously lying. She really believed she was sick; she had to. For the first time since knowing Sara, Dani actually felt sorry for her. "I hope you feel better in the morning, Sara," she said gently.

"If she doesn't," Mrs. G said, half to herself, "we'll have to take her to a doctor. Out in this wilderness, I wouldn't be surprised if the nearest one was on that Grey-suit's ship. What a mess. And on her birthday, too."

"And isn't that just typical," Karl muttered to Josh. "We've got important plans for tomorrow, and one way or another, Sara's bound to spoil them."

✧

In the hammock below Sara, Dani lay awake. Time travel. It didn't seem at all likely. The boys were going to try something, and they would probably fail, that was all. *Probably* fail. Okay, so there was a bare chance they wouldn't, but why should she care? Sara was always the one who cared, when the boys were trying to do things one better than them. If *Sara* didn't even want to know what Josh and Karl were up to . . .

But in any other situation she would have wanted to know. If she hadn't been so scared about going outside, Dani would have told her, and Sara would probably already have figured out a way to put a crimp in the boys' plans. Sara always said the boys shouldn't be allowed to win out over them just because they were older.

But probably all the boys would end up winning out on was getting some time to themselves that they'd waste. Fooling around with a bunch of old clocks, and nothing to show for it. . . .

They wouldn't go into the past. It was too silly to think about. Even Joshua was so unsure about the idea that he hadn't wanted to tell anybody, including Karl.

Then Dani remembered all those science projects of Josh's, his patent pending. She turned over in her hammock. That didn't mean he would always be right about everything scientific. But okay, just for the sake of argument, suppose Josh was right about time travel. Suppose they actually could go into the past, if they did the right thing to one of those clocks at the North Pole. Suppose she and Sara could get their hands on the right clock and do the right thing to it before the boys could. Then it would be the girls who would go into the past, not the boys.

If they went into the past at all. And they wouldn't. Almost certainly they wouldn't.

But if they could . . .

Dani sighed, rolled over again, and began twisting knots in her travel blanket.

The past. She tried to imagine it. A time where people came together by choice, not just because there was no room for them to be alone. Gardens, meadows, walks in a forest, drinking water from a well or even a river. Dani undid the knots in her blanket, then started another one, a giant this time. It would be wonderful to be outside in the sun without having to be protected by chemicals. And what if there were horses? Stallions with the wind in their manes, mares and colts nuzzling one another under fresh, mild skies . . . Dani stroked the knot in her blanket. She wanted to touch a horse, she wanted to pat its soft nose, to feel it nibble her palm for the sugar she would certainly be carrying, like the heroines in the televids.

Of course, it couldn't happen. The past was the past, finished, done with. You couldn't go there. It just wasn't possible.

But Josh thought he might be able to. He actually thought he might.

It was horrible to think that Josh and Karl might go into the past and see horses, and maybe not care enough even to notice. She was the only person she knew who wished there were open meadows left in the world for horses to roam. Not even up here in the Arctic with its

48

openness and freedom and its fresh wind blowing were there any horses running free.

What if Josh was right? What if he actually could go into the past, and take Karl with him?

If she was ever going to see horses anyplace but in a holograph or a televid or a zoo, it would be in the past.

Dani added another twist to her gigantic knot, then pushed the blanket away. She thought of prodding Sara awake and whispering out the whole story to her, but the four hammocks were so close together that one of the boys would be sure to wake and overhear. Anyway, if there was a time door at the North Pole, it was almost certain to be outside. What if Sara refused to go? What if that phobia thing Mrs. G had talked about kept Sara so afraid she might not *want* to go time traveling, even if she could?

Over in the pilot's chair Mrs. G was snoring gently. The blinking numbers on the pilot's datacenter told Dani it was two in the morning. She closed her eyes. Maybe if she slept on it, an idea would come to her. Sleep, she told herself sternly. Sleep.

But it was a long, long time before she did.

❖

"Happy birthday to me, happy birthday to me, happy birthday, dear Sara, happy birth—"

"Stuff it, Sara," Karl groaned sleepily, burying his head in his blanket.

Sara laughed, rolled out of her hammock, and dropped to the floor beside Dani, who was still sound asleep. It was her birthday, she was twelve years old, and that awful sick feeling she had had off and on all day yesterday was gone. Karl couldn't bother her today.

"Good morning, Grandma!" she called.

"Happy birthday, dear," Grandma said, smiling at her from the pilot's seat. "You're feeling better, I see. I was just lying here wondering whether it would be worthwhile putting together a birthday cake for you."

"I knew that unmarked packet was for me!"

"Can't have my only granddaughter turn twelve without a celebration."

"Do people really have to yell?" Joshua asked hollowly.

"Poor Josh," Sara said unsympathetically. "Didn't you sleep very well?"

"I think every bone in my back is broken," Josh grumbled. "Whoever said sleeping in a hammock was comfortable?"

"Try this pilot's chair, if you think *you're* sore," Grandma said. "Help me up, Sara, there's a good girl. I've got something I want to give you."

Sara grinned happily and tugged her grandmother upright. "A birthday present! What is it, Grandma?"

Her grandmother smiled. "It's in my jacket pocket, over there on the floor. Get it for me, will you?"

Sara handed her grandmother the jacket and watched excitedly as she took a small blue case from the pocket. "It looks like velvet," she breathed.

"It is. It's old, of course. You can't get velvet like this nowadays." She caressed the case for a moment, looking at Sara. "The thing inside isn't new, either. It was given to me on my twelfth birthday, and I thought you might like getting it on yours, too. I hope you will love it as much as I do."

Slowly, almost as if she didn't want to, she held the case out to Sara. Sara took it. "Is it jewelry?" she asked hesitantly. Somehow she didn't want to look inside the case.

"Open it and see."

"Dani should be watching when I do."

"She's dead to the world," Grandma said. "And I can't wait. Open it, dear."

Sara smiled nervously, then pried the case open. Inside was a gold chain with a large pendant hanging from it. The pendant was a spherical crystal with many glittering facets on the outside and a hollow space on the inside. The hollow space wasn't empty. Inside it was a miniature of a wilderness scene, a tiny maple tree beside a silver lake, a bird floating on the water. There were leaves on the tree, black-and-white feathers on the bird, ripples on the water. Sara took the chain in one hand and held it up to the light. Every facet of the crystal showed a different aspect of the little scene. Every aspect was perfect.

"Exquisite, isn't it?" Grandma said. "Entirely hand-made, of course. They wouldn't know how to do something like that nowadays."

"It's great, Grandma," Sara said. She tried to smile as gratefully as she knew the pendant deserved. "Thank you very much."

Grandma's clever blue eyes narrowed a little. Sara looked away from them. She knew she ought to like the pendant more than she did. Obviously it was very, very valuable. And she could see that to her grandmother its value was more than just the money it had cost. Sara didn't dislike it, but it made her feel strange. That perfect vision of a long-ago Earth didn't belong here. It was inside the puffhover, closed away from the open spaces of the Arctic, and it was inside that crystal, too, yet Sara thought it couldn't have been more outside if it were a real scene and she were in it.

"The bird is a loon," Grandma said. "See the tiny red eyes, and that black cap, and the two patches of black and white stripes on its neck? We had loons on my lake

51

when I was your age. They used to call to each other—like the saddest laugh you've ever heard. . . ." She sighed, then smiled at Sara. "Do you want to try it on? The chain was broken once, a long time ago. We got it mended, but you can still see the join."

The slight thickening of two or three links of the fine gold chain didn't bother Sara at all. It was the pendant she minded, not the chain. Her grandmother was eyeing her anxiously. Sara cleared her throat. "Grandma, why are you giving me something you still love so much?"

"Maybe I don't need it anymore," Grandma said oddly. "Maybe I think you do."

Sara stared at her uncomprehendingly for a moment, then let her turn her around to fasten the clasp under her long red hair. "Thanks, Grandma," Sara said. "I really like it."

The lie felt awkward on her tongue. As casually as she could she put the pendant under her UV-shirt where it rested against the tunic beneath. "Too fragile to risk while I'm cooking," she explained, and managed to give the lump under her shirt a loving pat. Grandma turned away. Sara was pretty sure she hadn't been fooled.

She was angry suddenly. She needed all kinds of things —a pair of dance blades, a new leotard, rollergloves, a helmet— and what did her grandmother give her? A crystal that was no more than a piece of her darned Grassroots propaganda, an outside thing that had nothing to do with rollergyms or the twenty-first century or anything that Sara cared about at all. And then, she had to go and make Sara feel guilty about not liking it as much as she'd expected her to.

Sara grabbed a package of freeze-dried pancakes, went over to the microwave, and spent the next few minutes beating out her frustration on a bowl.

Chapter Five

THEY left right after breakfast. Grandma kept the floor window closed. "We're in turbo most of the way," she explained, "and there isn't anything to see but ocean anyway."

Sara didn't care why Grandma kept the window closed. She was just glad that she did. She settled herself into her straps and closed her eyes, listening to the whir of the puffhover's pads and the comforting hum of the artificial light. If it hadn't been for Dani, shifting uncomfortably in the seat beside her, she might almost have been able to relax. But Dani was bothered about something, and Sara knew it. She had wanted to tell Sara a secret ever since last night, and Sara hadn't let her. I couldn't go outside with her, Sara told herself for at least the tenth time. It's not my fault there's nowhere private to talk in the puffhover. But still she felt guilty.

When they went turbo, she didn't have to think. But it was a different matter when they came out of it again. The North Pole was close. Every minute it was getting closer. People would be wanting to go outside again once they got there. Dani would, certainly.

Sara slid her fingers in and out of the rollergloves Dani had given her this morning. They were her favorite present, though even Josh and Karl had remembered her birthday. Josh had designed her a card with her name in lasercuts, and Karl had got her a wrist guard for archery. It was an old one he had found in a recycling shop, but it looked like real leather, and it was something Sara had wanted for ages. But when she'd thanked him, really pleased, he'd only grunted, "Maybe it'll help you hit the target now and then." In all the fuss, Sara hadn't mentioned Grandma's pendant to anyone, and neither had Grandma.

Dani had been extra nice to Sara this morning, hugging her from behind as she poured out the pancake batter and wishing her a happy birthday several times. She didn't say a word about last night. But she would want to go outside again when they got to the North Pole. And she, and Grandma, and everybody else, would want Sara to go with them.

The North Pole. Almost, Sara wanted to go. The North Pole was special, not like that no-man's-land they'd spent the afternoon at yesterday. People had tried to get to the North Pole for hundreds of years; some had even died trying. It was something you made up stories about. A place of adventure. Sara liked adventure. And it was her birthday. What a thing to remember, when it was all over, that she had spent her twelfth birthday at the North Pole.

But it was outside. Her stomach turned queasy at the thought.

"What will there be when we get there, Mrs. G?" Dani asked.

"Pack ice," Josh said, speaking for Grandma, who was punching numbers into the navicomp.

"Ice? But it's so warm up here," Dani protested.

"The ice everywhere in the Arctic is thinner than it used to be," Grandma said, looking up, "but the Pole is in the middle of a fairly solid bit."

"We *can* stand on the actual Pole, can't we?" Karl asked anxiously.

"Yes, unless my Greysuit's ordered his icebreaker to break things up just there."

At this Josh sat up. "Why would he do that?" he demanded. "Not to drill for oil, surely! The North Pole is international. Nobody private can—"

"I didn't say they'd put an oil rig there," Grandma said. "Not that Adam Duguay wouldn't want to do it if he could. Most of the oil under the Arctic Ocean is too far down to get at, but there is an underwater ridge that runs directly beneath the North Pole, and the water there is only three to four kilometers deep. That's not too deep for modern oil rigs if you really want oil."

"And Adam Duguay really wants it?" Karl asked soberly.

"A lot of people really want it," Grandma said.

"But we don't burn it anymore," Dani said.

"It's still used for expensive goods like plastiques." Grandma was silent a moment. Then, very seriously, she added, "There's a lot of money at stake here. Duguay will put oil rigs shoulder to shoulder all along that ridge, cutting the Arctic in two, if he gets his way. Have you any idea what even one uncapped gusher can do to an isolated, enclosed sea like the one we're flying over? The last nearly clean sea remaining on the face of this Earth?"

No one said anything for a moment or two. Then Karl asked, "What are you going to do, Grandma?"

"I'm going to stop him," his grandmother replied.

"Can you?"

"That's what I was spending all last month in the law archives and most of last night at the computer working out," Grandma said. "And now, you lot, stop asking questions until I get us down."

"You mean, we're here? We're at the North Pole?"

"Almost right over it," Grandma said.

Sara's fingers gripped the arms of her seat. She watched as her grandmother keyed in a series of commands to the navicomp. The hoverpads changed sound. Grandma pressed a button, and the floor covering slid out of sight. Light flooded into the puffhover from below. Sara sat back in her chair, staring straight ahead.

"I see the Greysuit's icebreaker!" Karl exclaimed. "Is it ever big!"

"Big enough to cover the North Pole," Grandma said wryly.

"You mean it's anchored right over it?" Josh demanded, outraged.

"It is."

"But my experiments—he can't be—you have to get him to move!"

"I've got oil rigs to worry about," Grandma said, "and they're more important than your experiments, Josh. If I start off by asking Duguay a favor, I lose the advantage. You wouldn't want that."

"But—"

"No buts," Grandma said sternly. "Be quiet now. I'm going to voice-link with them."

✧

While Mrs. G made the connection, Dani looked out of the viewing window. The puffhover was hanging rather low over a blue-grey jostle of ice floes and water some distance away from the icebreaker. The round viewport showed the icebreaker's lingering effects: a fair amount of open water, with ice piled floe on floe like shards of broken porcelain. Where the sun shone on it the ice took on the livid glow of a bruise. Here and there a wave, larger than usual, broke against an ice floe with a huge white splash.

"*Grassroots Three* calling icebreaker *Seabeater*, *Grassroots Three* to *Seabeater*, come in, please." Mrs. G's voice sounded so professional that Dani almost didn't recognize it.

Over the loudspeaker of the commsystem, a man's voice was heard. "*Seabeater* here. Your pilot, please, *Grassroots Three*."

"You're speaking to her," Mrs. G said. "Give me Duguay."

"Name?"

"Duguay, please." Mrs. G. winked at Dani.

"*Your* name."

"He'll know, Commofficer. He'll also know who kept me waiting if you don't get him on this phone, pronto."

Cool, Dani thought admiringly, very cool, very tough.

Another man's voice came over the loudspeaker. "Chief Justice Green, I assume?"

"Ex—chief justice, Mr. Duguay. I haven't been on the bench for quite some time. But you can call me Counselor if you like."

"Then you are here on a legal matter after all?" The man's voice was smooth, unsurprised. "We thought perhaps you were just sight-seeing."

"Mr. Duguay, I use a Grassroots puffhover only when I'm on business."

"With four children on board?"

"How does he know?" Karl asked.

"Shh," Josh whispered. "He's been spying on us, obviously."

"You're never too young to learn Grassroots business," Mrs. G said perfectly calmly. "As well, two of my crew are young scientists, here to do some experiments at the North Pole."

57

"I'm afraid *Seabeater* has rather taken up residence over the Pole. But if your young scientists need to be where we are, they're welcome to come and do their experiments on board."

"Yes!" Josh whispered exultantly.

Mrs. G frowned at him and shook her head slightly. "What I had in mind was your coming here, Mr. Duguay."

The man waited a moment. Dani guessed why. He would naturally prefer to have his discussions with Mrs. G on his own territory. At last he said, "Puffhovers are so cramped. But I suppose, if your crew came on board my ship, there would be enough room for the two of us in your puffhover. It seems a fair exchange: four of them for one of me."

Clever Mrs. G! Dani thought. To make the man give her what she wanted, and what the boys wanted, too, and all without appearing to have given anything away herself at all! Duguay had put a good face on it, though, Dani had to admit. *Four of them for one of me.* Sort of like hostages, Dani thought. Then something else occurred to her. Mrs. G would never let the four of them out of her sight on a Greysuit's ship without ordering them to stay together. And that meant that the boys were not going to be able to do their time experiments without witnesses. Dani hugged herself.

The boys had figured it out, too. Josh was biting his lip in frustration, and Karl was glaring at Sara and Dani alternately, just as if what had been agreed between his grandmother and Mr. Duguay was their fault.

Dani didn't care. She sent a sparkling glance Sara's way, but her friend was only sitting back in her chair, staring dully at her grandmother. Of course. She didn't want to go outside. But she was going to have to. This time, she was going to have to. And she knew it.

Dani knew exactly what her friend was thinking. Sara couldn't get sick again. If she did, Mrs. G would be sure to send her to be checked out by the doctor who was bound to be on that huge icebreaker over there. Either way, she was going to have to go outside.

"You'll come aboard with the children first, Counselor?" Adam Duguay was going on. "I'll have my chef prepare something special. I believe your granddaughter is having a birthday today. A feast of sorts might be in order."

Dani's eyes widened. This man knew too much. It was almost scary.

"I'm planning my own feast for Sara, Mr. Duguay. And you faxed me that you didn't have very much time to devote to our discussions. I'll bring the children over and see them settled, but after that I think you and I should come right back here."

Sara was still staring at her grandmother. Dani felt sorry for her. But once she got a chance to explain to Sara about the time traveling, that would distract her from her fear of being outside. It would get her thinking, too. There was nothing like being mad at the boys for making Sara come up with plans.

Chapter Six

THE Greysuit called Adam Duguay stood at the lee rail of the icebreaker, watching the dinghy making its approach through the churning, ice-strewn water that separated the puffhover from the anchored ship. He was alone. That had surprised Dani. She would have thought he'd be surrounded by servants or something. And he wasn't wearing a grey suit. Dani had observed that at once, although the way the inflatable dinghy bounced it was hard to keep anything on the bigger ship in sight for more than a second at a time.

The sky was overcast, with the look of rain to come. Where the dinghy drove through the tops of tossing wavelets a fine, icy spray arose, turning instantly to steam in the warm wind. Miniature ice floes slid into one another with eerie creaks and groans, but the sailor from the *Seabeater* was an expert pilot and the dinghy was never in danger of running into anything.

The sea was rougher than Dani had expected. Because of the weather Mrs. G had decided not to bring the little craft down onto the water, but instead had left it resting on a calm cushion of air, just above the waves. That had made it more interesting, getting into the dinghy from the portastairs, but the sailor had been there to steady them.

The whole way to the icebreaker, Karl and Josh fidgeted, now and then muttering quietly to each other in the front of the little boat. Dani couldn't hear what they said, but she guessed they were trying to figure out how to get away from her and Sara once the four of them were alone on the icebreaker. She looked hopefully at Sara, sitting beside her in the middle of the dinghy. No one would hear a whisper over the noise the little dinghy was making. She could tell Sara what the boys were up to if she could only get her to stop thinking about being outside. But Sara was stony faced, staring grimly into her lap.

On Sara's other side Mrs. G was quietly observing the Greysuit, who was dressed in casual pants and a long-sleeved white shirt, open at the neck. It was a warm day, too hot for a zipsuit, really; but still, Dani was surprised that Adam Duguay wouldn't be wearing the prescribed Arctic outfit, even if not a grey suit. Surreptitiously she unzipped the collar and top third of her own suit and let her hood drop. Immediately she felt more comfortable. She turned to Sara, who seemed to be breathing very shallowly. "Open your suit," Dani said to her. "You'll feel better." Sara turned a wide-eyed, white face to her. Gently Dani reached around and unzipped Sara's suit halfway to her waist, then pushed off the hood. "There. Isn't that cooler?"

Sara said nothing, but at least she was looking at her now. This was her chance. Dani whispered, "Sara, you know how Josh said all the time zones in the world meet at—?"

"No," Sara said, turning her face away.

Dani blinked, then tugged at Sara's arm. "But the boys think they might be able to use a clock to—"

"Dani, please."

"They're going to try to—"

"I don't care what they do," Sara said miserably. Her eyes were fixed on her lap as if it were the only reliable thing in the entire universe. Hoarsely she added, "I'm sorry, Dani. I can't. Just don't talk, okay?"

Hurt, Dani subsided. She tried to imagine how Sara must be feeling, scared of being outside and then stuck out here in a tiny open boat with this vast ocean all around.

Seabeater was growing closer and closer. Duguay was still standing at the rail, smiling calmly down at them. He had a craggy face with prominent cheekbones and eyebrows, but the thick grey hair whipping around his head and that smile he was sending down to them softened the angles in his face, making him look almost pleasant. Dani thought his alert grey gaze went more with his cheekbones than with that smile. She thought he might be the kind of man who would give Mrs. G as much trouble as she gave him.

As the sailor brought the dinghy under *Seabeater*'s lee side, the note of the engine changed, then stopped altogether. Someone threw a rope to the sailor, who caught it expertly and tied it to a cleat in the stern. He scrambled forward and another rope came from the icebreaker. The sailor tied it to the bow. They were secure now, hugged into the side of the huge icebreaker and protected by its bulk from the waves and the ice on its weather side.

A door slid open about a third of the way up the ship's side, revealing a uniformed woman. "Heads!" she called, and a long set of portastairs descended. Dani ducked at the woman's warning, though there was really no need. When the stairs stopped falling, the bottom step was no lower than the sailor's waist. He roped it to a cleat in the side of the icebreaker. "All set now," he said to Josh and Karl, who were nearest. "You two need a hoist up?"

Karl gave him a look of offended dignity, then said pointedly to Josh, "I'll go first. You can pass me up your bag after."

One by one they pulled themselves up onto the portastairs, then ascended to the opening in the icebreaker's side. When it was Sara's turn she cast a despairing look at her grandmother, then half leaped, half dragged herself onto the portastairs and began scrambling up as quickly as if a murderer were coming after her. Dani followed, trying to catch up to her. But she never could go as fast as Sara, and when her friend finally fled after Josh and Karl through the open door, there was nobody above Dani at all until Adam Duguay appeared in the opening.

"Welcome aboard," he said as she struggled up the top two steps.

"Hello," she said shyly, peering into the brightly lit interior of the plastique-clad room behind him. It was empty, but a door stood open on its other side.

"Your friends are up on deck," he said. "I've got someone directing them to the North Pole."

"Isn't it under us?"

"It's only a point. The ship is bigger than it is." He smiled and jerked his head toward the door opposite, but his eyes were on Mrs. G, behind Dani on the portastairs. "That way," he said, "and up the first set of stairs you see."

Dani cast a quick glance backward, but Mrs. G only smiled up at her and waved. Dani nodded. Mrs. G could take care of herself. "Thanks," she said to the Greysuit, and ran.

✧

The first flight of stairs was a long climb, especially after the portastairs, and Dani was out of breath by the time she reached the top. Sara was sitting huddled into herself on the last step. The boys were nowhere to be seen.

"I can't go out there," Sara said drearily when Dani stopped beside her.

"Sara, the boys are going to try to time travel into the past. That's what Josh's experiment with clocks is all about. And if we don't do something, they're going to try it without us!"

"Who cares?"

Dani stared at her, aghast. She had expected amazement, even disbelief, not that dull, careless "Who cares?"

"I'd rather not talk business here," came Mrs. G's voice.

Dani turned in relief. Mrs. G and the Greysuit were on the stairs behind them, only a short distance away. Mrs. G wouldn't let Sara sit on the stairs while the boys did their experiments. Sara seemed to know it, too. She stood up, her eyes huge. The movement attracted Mrs. G's attention. She looked up, frowning.

"Were you waiting for us, you two? I thought I told you to stick with the boys."

"We lost track of them," Dani said swiftly. "It's a big ship. We didn't know which way to go."

Mr. Duguay answered, "They'll be over on the windward side, toward the bow. That's where you'll find the exact position of the North Pole. I'll take you."

He took Dani's arm. She didn't seem to have a choice. Sara followed, with Mrs. G beside her. Together they came out of the covered stairwell onto the open deck. They were about halfway between the bow and the stern of the huge vessel, protected from the worst of the wind by a large plastiqued storage locker and a rack of lifeboats. Knots of busy-looking people were overhauling a thick cable that had been laid out on the deck on the leeward side. There was no sign of the boys.

The four of them crossed the deck to the other side, then turned toward the bow, Dani still arm in arm with the Greysuit. Now they were out of the shelter of the lifeboat rack and could feel the wind, strong and warm and capricious as an animal. Despite its strength, it was oddly noiseless. Dani supposed that there was nothing up here in the Arctic for the wind to make a noise against, except for *Seabeater* herself. She squinted out to sea. Everything was the same color, a bruised-looking violet grey. There was no horizon, only water, ice, and sky all blending. Almost with relief she caught sight of a flock of birds fleeing before the wind like little dark bullets. She turned her head to follow them and saw Mrs. G watching them, too. "Storm petrels," Mrs. G said. "Looks as if they're living up to their name today."

Dani turned her eyes toward the bow. There were Josh and Karl. They were protected from the wind, standing in front of another rack of lifeboats, doing something with Josh's softpack of clocks. They looked as if they were arguing. "If they need to be right over the North Pole," Duguay said to Dani, "they're in the wrong place. The Pole is just this side of that lifeboat rack. Do you think it matters?"

She nodded, mutely. He smiled. "Then we'd better tell them," he said cheerfully.

They marched down the deck, Sara crowding up behind Dani, who was feeling so uncomfortable with her arm imprisoned in this Greysuit's grasp and her hair whipping across her face that she hardly noticed. On her other side and slightly ahead now was Mrs. G, her eyes turned seaward.

"This is it," Duguay said, stopping at a faint chalk mark on the deck.

"The North Pole?" Dani asked.

"The captain had a survey done. I chalked this mark myself afterward. I like knowing exactly where things are."

"Mrs. G," Dani called.

But Mrs. G's mind was elsewhere. "Listen," she said suddenly.

"What is it?" Dani asked.

"That sound—like laughing—"

"I don't hear—" Dani broke off. She *could* hear something. It was distant, hollow, like laughter but too clear and too high. "What is it?"

"Listen."

They all stood still. Down the deck from them the boys watched, frowning. Dani could hear Karl ask, "What's with them?" She could also hear that same high-pitched laughter, farther away now, echoing and sad.

"It's a loon," Mrs. G said excitedly. She reached for the railing and leaned out, searching the sky feverishly. "I'm sure of it. Can anyone see it? It's a loon, I'm sure it is!"

For a long moment they all stood quietly, listening and looking. But the loon was gone. Slowly, sadly, Mrs. G turned away.

"Loons used to be on coins," Duguay said, "didn't they?"

"That was when they hadn't all died out everywhere in the south."

"What happened to them, Mrs. G?" Dani asked.

"Pollution. Hunters. The usual." She shrugged. "I haven't seen or heard one since I was twelve. But apparently some still remain up here in the Arctic." She shook

67

her hair back, lifting her chin challengingly at Adam Duguay. "Just where you want to erect your oil rigs."

Duguay's eyes narrowed. "Can't say I've ever seen a loon myself. Pretty birds, are they?"

"Show him, Sara. The birthday present I gave you."

Dani turned to Sara in surprise. Mrs. G. had given Sara a present but her friend hadn't told her.

Sara was staring downward, her shoulders hunched. She didn't seem to have heard her grandmother's request. "I asked you to show Mr. Duguay your pendant, Sara," Mrs. G. said.

"I don't want to." It was a mutter, barely audible.

Mrs. G gave an annoyed laugh. "Really, Sara. If you don't like it enough—"

Sara looked up then. Her eyes blazed suddenly. "Yes, Grandma. Whatever you say, Grandma. Do this, do that, go to the Arctic, go outside." White-faced and furious, she fumbled under her UV-shirt and pulled something out, then made a fist around it and shoved it in the general direction of Adam Duguay's face, gold chain dangling. "Mr. Duguay, sir, do please look at my pendant." She turned her fist palm up and opened her fingers.

Duguay looked at Mrs. G's stony expression, then at Sara. As if not quite certain what to do, he leaned forward. "Very nice," he said.

"Look at it properly," Sara commanded. "The loon's very small. Grandma wants you to look at it."

Again Mr. Duguay sent a questioning look to Mrs. G, and again he got no help. Tentatively, he reached out a finger, hooked the chain under it, and pulled the pendant toward him.

What happened next, Dani never knew. Maybe the icebreaker shifted. Maybe Sara involuntarily jerked her hand backward at the man's touch. Maybe he pulled the chain too hard. Or maybe, just maybe, Sara did what she did deliberately.

Whatever caused it, Dani was perfectly certain of the results. She saw it all, sharp-etched moments like freeze-frame photography. Tiny movements rippling one after the other, everything slowing down, the gold chain stretching taut, the links bending, her own free hand reaching forward, slowly, so slowly, to clutch Sara's wrist. Man and girl and chain and girl, entangled and joined in the slowness of everything, gold links twisting — slower and slower — then opening, oozing apart, a glittering shower frozen against a violet sky —

And then, nothing.

Chapter Seven

I T was warm. Dani opened her eyes, stared in bewilderment, closed them again. No. She hadn't seen what she thought she'd seen. She was at the North Pole, on the deck of an icebreaker. Sara was there, and Mrs. G, and the Greysuit, and the boys; from the deck of the ship you could see ice, water, a few birds, clouds fleeing before the wind. What you did not see was trees, an old-fashioned house built on huge pink boulders, or a canoe being paddled over a sparkling lake by bareheaded blond kids. And you definitely did not have your hand tightly closed on the soft sleeve of some strange girl's arm, while that girl used *her* hand to jerk at a gold chain hooked by a man's index finger.

"You broke it. You did it on purpose!"

A man's voice, hurt and astonished. Dani had never heard that voice before in her life. She opened her eyes again. The strange girl was still there. So was the man. So were the trees, and the rocks, and the house, and the lake. A rickety wooden structure rocked beneath her feet, and there was sunlight on her head and a green smell in her nostrils. Moving only her head, Dani looked from one strange sight to the next, back and forth, back and forth, her heart pounding in her ears. Where was she? How had she got here? *Who were these people?*

"I'm ashamed of you, Gwen Thompson!" There was anger in the man's voice now, along with the hurt and surprise. He had a dimple in his left cheek just like the girl's, but as Dani watched, it disappeared, ironed out by

71

the frown that made a solid vee out of his dark brows. "Your mother told me you loved this pendant. She said you kept going back to that jewelry store in Toronto to look at it. And now, when I've finally bought it for you, you go and—"

"Do you think I'm too stupid to figure out why you bought it for me?" The girl—Gwen Thompson, Dani reminded herself—shook her blond hair back and lifted her chin defiantly at him. It was a vaguely familiar gesture. Dani clutched Gwen's sleeve more tightly.

"I got it for you because you are my daughter and it's your birthday and I love you."

"I know how much it cost. I'm not a baby, Dad, I'm twelve. Five thousand dollars. Where'd you get five thousand dollars?" The girl's fist opened and let go of the thing that had been hidden there. Her arm, the one Dani was gripping, dropped to her side. Dani's dropped with it, but neither the girl nor the man seemed to notice Dani's presence. Both of them were watching the chain that now hung loose on Mr. Thompson's index finger. It began to slide toward the ground, pulled by the weight of a large crystal pendant that had been hidden in Gwen's fist. The man caught at it and closed his fingers around the pendant.

"That's right," he said bitterly. "Five thousand dollars. The most expensive gift I've ever been able to buy you, so naturally you break it the minute I give it to you."

"Two weeks ago you couldn't find five *hundred* dollars to repair this dock." She stamped on the wooden structure beneath their feet, her blue eyes glittering. "Where did you find five thousand? As if I didn't know!"

I shouldn't be here, Dani thought suddenly. This is private. However I got here, I should leave now.

But that would mean letting go of Gwen's arm. Dani didn't want to do that. There was something about the other girl's arm that felt real to her, something familiar underneath all the foreignness. Dani felt that if she let go of it she would be lost.

She cleared her throat uncertainly, trying to draw their attention to apologize for her presence. Neither Mr. Thompson nor Gwen looked at her. It was as if Dani weren't even there. Dani felt frightened suddenly. *Was* she there? Or was she dreaming this whole thing? She looked down at her hand, saw it clutching Gwen's arm, felt the tension of the girl's muscles and the odd familiarity deep beneath them. How could something *inside* another person be familiar when the outside was a complete stranger?

"So *that's* it," Mr. Thompson said. He sounded tired, suddenly. "You heard about the mill. Who told you? Your mother? I was going to tell you, Gwennie, truly I was. I was just waiting till after your birthday. I know how much you love this place—"

"How much did the lumber people give you?" Gwen demanded. "A million dollars? Two?"

"It's none of your business."

"None of my business?" she asked. Her voice shook. "I don't live here, then?"

"Yes, you live here. But you don't know what it's been like these last years. Trying to make ends meet on fewer and fewer lodge rentals and the odd fishing party—and everything costing so much . . ." Gwen turned her head away, refusing to look at him. His voice changed. "Look, I don't have to ask anybody's permission to sell my own land."

"And the lake, too. Don't forget the lake."

Gwen's whole body was shaking now. Dani could feel it. Helplessly she stood there, her hand glued to this stranger's arm, while two people she didn't know argued furiously in front of her. I should go, she told herself again. I should just step back out of this and go.

"I heard my loons again this morning," Gwen ground out, still with her head turned away. "They were calling to each other here, just before dawn. Do you think they'll stick around when the mill goes up?"

"I *gave* you a loon, Gwen," the man said caustically, shoving the hand that held the crystal pendant in her face so that even Dani could see. "You broke it."

Another girl besides Sara with a loon pendant, Dani thought. Where *was* Sara? Oh, if only she were here! But she wasn't. Nothing normal was here, only this foreign place full of trees and rocks and sunlight and lake, those blond-headed kids, this girl, this man ... Panic filled Dani. Where was she? Why was she here? And why, why was she all alone?

"I have to get out of here," she said aloud. "I have to get back!" She knew she said it aloud. She almost yelled it. But neither Gwen nor her father seemed to hear.

"Yes, you gave me a loon," Gwen said. "And I did love it in the store, because it made me think of my real loons on my real lake. But the real loons will go away when the mill goes up. The trees will be gone, and the lake will be full of chemicals, and the only things alive here will be people who love money. How could you think that a pendant could make up to me for that? How *could* you?"

"We'll move away," Mr. Thompson said. "We'll find another lake."

"There isn't anything you can do," Gwen said, slowly and distinctly, "that'll ever make up for this."

"Gwen—"

The girl swept regally around him. Helplessly, Dani felt herself go with her. Then Gwen began to run, and Dani, still holding tight to the girl's arm, was flying along with her. I'm not moving my feet, Dani thought blankly. I'm running, and I'm not moving my feet.

Trees sped by, sharp scented, scratchy. Up a path, one of Gwen's feet catching on a root, Dani hanging on grimly. She made herself concentrate on her hand, that solid stubby right hand that she'd known her whole life, a hand that could belong to no one but herself. She could see it, white knuckled, gripping the blue cloth of Gwen's sleeve. That hand—*her* hand—was there. She could feel it, and feel with it; it was *there*. And if it was there, so was she; all of her, whether or not she was running with her feet, whether or not Gwen noticed another person beside her on the path, whether or not it was possible for her to be there at all. She *was* there.

Thud. Thud. Thud. Thud. Feet pounding on moss-covered stones, up and up, rhythmic as one of Joshua's ticking clocks. "Hate him," Gwen gasped to herself, over and over, as repetitive as her footsteps. "—hate him, hate him, hate him." The big old house angled into view, doors and windows wide open, someone waving at Gwen from one of them. Gwen didn't look. She only ran, her breath coming in sobs, and the house disappeared behind them.

Disappeared. Panic rose again in Dani. She had been on a perfectly ordinary icebreaker, and it had disappeared. The North Pole had disappeared. Sara and Mrs. G and the boys had disappeared. So had Mr. Duguay. How safe was this place, this girl? How safe was Dani herself?

"—never forgive him, never!"

Branches, scratching Gwen's face. One of them whipped Dani's; she felt it, but it didn't hurt.

Maybe I'm asleep, Dani thought. Maybe I'm still in my hammock on the puffhover, and all this is just a dream.

Down on her knees, crawling beside Gwen. A gorgeous, rich smell, the pure odor of green.

Nothing smells like a color, Dani told herself. It has to be a dream.

Shadows. A hole, no, a hiding place: a scented dim retreat at the foot of a giant evergreen, branches overhead and all around, even the sky gone away. Gwen threw herself on the ground, spent; then she made a final effort and curled herself around the trunk, hugging it to her and panting harshly.

I want to wake up, Dani thought.

Time passed, a long time. Gwen fell asleep. Dani didn't.

How can I fall asleep when I'm asleep already? she asked herself reasonably.

More time passed. Wake up! she told herself.

But still she lay beside Gwen, still with her hand on her sleeve. Outside somewhere, a bird trilled. A different one answered it. So many birds, Dani thought. So many trees. And a lake that was as clear as crystal, fresh air to breathe, people bareheaded and fearless in the warm sun, a big shabby house that was obviously meant for ordinary people to live in. Not a blockbuilding or a robot or a puffhover in sight; plenty of space to get away from other people when you wanted to; a world where you could be alone.

It felt so real.

Think, Dani told herself. Think.

76

Two broken chains. Gwen's here. Sara's at the North Pole—the *exact* North Pole.

Josh had said you could time travel at the exact North Pole. He had said you'd need a kind of key to open the time door there. A clock, he'd thought.

What if it were Sara's birthday pendant instead?

Another bird began to sing, a long, lovely melody. Dani lay in the tree's green shadows and listened. There were no birds or trees like this in the twenty-first century. There was nothing like this in her own time at all.

But in the *past* there had been places like this. If this was the past, if Joshua's key really had been Sara's birthday pendant, if breaking it had opened a North Pole time door and for some reason had sent Dani alone through that door . . .

Yes. It made sense.

She was in the past. There was no way around it. She had never felt so lonely in her life.

"Sara," Dani whispered. "Oh, Sara, I wish you were with me."

"Dani?"

Dani's heart almost stopped. She jerked upright, her hand pulling away from Gwen's blue sleeve. If she had thought of it, she might not have dared to let go of the thing she had begun to think of as a kind of anchor, but it made no difference. She was still here, still in this dim little hidey-hole, still alone.

"Dani? Why don't you answer me? I know it's dark, but if I can hear you, you can hear me."

Frantically, Dani peered around her, but there was no one there, only Gwen, curled into the tree, sleeping. It was impossible. Sara was here. But it was impossible!

"I—Sara? Is that you? It doesn't quite sound like your voice, but—"

77

"Of course it's me, idiot. Who else would it be?"

Dani gave a little cry of joy. "Oh, Sara, where are you? I can't see you!"

"What do you expect, in the middle of the night? But wait a minute. I was on the icebreaker, and then I was asleep. How — ? And it was morning. Now it's pitch-dark. . . ."

"It's not that dark. It's not the middle of the night, either. I don't understand why you — " She broke off. "Shh. Gwen's turning over in her sleep."

"Who's Gwen?"

"She's—" Dani stopped suddenly. She stared at Gwen, who now was lying on her back, pale eyelashes fanned against the unnatural brown of her cheeks. Her mouth was open. "Sara?" Dani got out, her voice trembling.

"What? Hey, Dani, don't be scared, we're together, it's okay."

Dani gave a soundless moan. Her hands flew up to cover her mouth. It was Sara who spoke, but it had been Gwen's lips that had moved.

"Is that Gwen person still here? Why can't I see her? Who is she?"

Dani stared, and stared.

"Dani?" Panicky, now. "Are you still here? I asked you who Gwen was."

"Who's Gwen?" Dani got out at last. She laughed, a ghost of a laugh, almost a cry. "You are," she said, and the truth was in her voice, incontestable. "Oh, Sara, you are."

✧

"I understand how my breaking my pendant could have brought me back to a time when somebody else broke her pendant," Sara said thoughtfully. "But I don't get it

78

that I ended up inside that person, instead of being free like you."

"I don't feel free," Dani said. "I feel like a ghost."

"Don't be an idiot, Dani. You're not a ghost. You're just not inside somebody else."

Dani was silent. How could she explain the horrible feeling of not being there for other people, of not mattering? "They couldn't see me at all," she said. "Gwen and her father, I mean. They couldn't hear me either. It was horrible, Sara. I could see myself, and hear myself, but until you spoke to me, I might have been alone in the universe."

"Maybe Gwen and her dad were just too busy yelling at each other to notice anything else. I'll bet other people will be able to see you just fine."

"I ran without moving my feet," Dani said, almost in a whisper. "A branch hit me in the face, and it didn't even hurt."

"But you knew it had hit you, right?"

"Yes," Dani said hopefully.

"Can you move around by yourself?"

Dani got to her knees. Her head brushed the lowest overhanging branch. She put her hand on it, rubbing the rough bark, feeling the stickiness of the resin. Then she examined her fingers, trying to see if any of the resin had come off. But it was too dim in Gwen's little hidey-hole to be sure.

"Well?" Sara asked impatiently.

"Yes, I can move," Dani said, slumping back to the ground and hugging her knees to her chest, fiercely glad that they still looked and felt so solid and real.

"You see? Free to go where you want when you want. You're ten times as lucky as me, stuck in this Gwen person's body."

Dani thought about this, amazed how quickly she'd gotten used to Gwen lying there sound asleep while Sara, inside Gwen's body, was wide-awake and talking. "Maybe real time travel works like that," she suggested. "Maybe if you go back in time because you happen to repeat an action somebody else did once, then you have to become that other person."

"In all the time-travel televids I've seen," Sara said, "people who go back in time get to stay in their own bodies. It'd be a lot more fun than just lying here while this Gwen girl snores."

"She's not really snoring," Dani said. "You couldn't be talking if she were."

"Oh, you know what I mean."

Dani was thinking hard. "I saw a televid once," she said slowly, "where a man went back in time and stepped on a butterfly. Then, when he tried to go back to his own time, he couldn't. His own time wasn't there anymore because he'd killed that butterfly."

"That sounds dumb," Sara said.

"No, it made sense, really. A whole bunch of things happened because of the butterfly dying, one thing causing the next, and each new thing getting bigger and more important, until finally the whole path of history changed, and the man's future no longer existed."

"So where did he come from, then?"

"I see what you mean." Dani thought for a long moment. "So maybe the only way you can really go back in time is if you *can't* do something while you're in the past that would change the whole course of history. But bodies are always doing something. So for us to come into the past, either we can't have a body at all — like me, or —"

"Or—like me—we have to be inside someone who actually lived in the past," Sara finished for her. Her words came slowly, as if she were figuring it out as she went. "*I* get Gwen's body because she and I both broke the loon pendants. That connected us, I guess. But you don't get a body at all, because when Gwen broke her loon pendant there wasn't another girl beside her with her hand on her arm the way you had yours on mine."

Dani nodded. "And if we're right that we can't change the course of history," she said thoughtfully, "then Gwen'll have to keep on doing the things she would have done before we got here."

"That's just great. What if she's really boring? What if she sleeps all the time, or eats horrible things, or has to practice the keyboard for five hours a day?"

"It's better than not being anybody," Dani said.

"All because of the stupid coincidence of us both breaking the same kind of pendant," Sara said gloomily. Her voice changed. "Wait a minute. Didn't you say Josh thought the key to the North Pole time door would likely be something that existed in both times? Ours, and the past, I mean."

"That's why he wanted to use an old clock," Dani agreed.

"It does make sense," Sara said excitedly. "Why should my breaking any old pendant take me back in time to when Gwen broke a different one? But if they were the same pendant . . ."

"But how could Gwen break your brand-new pendant?" Dani asked bewilderedly.

"It isn't brand-new. It was Grandma's for a long time before she gave it to me. She got it for her twelfth birthday. And Dani, *Gwen* got the pendant for her twelfth birthday, too."

81

"Are you saying—?"

"Gwen broke her chain, Dani, we know that. And Grandma told me her chain was broken once, too. And Grandma lived on a lake when she was young. Gwen lives on a lake." Sara was breathless with excitement now. "Gwen—Gwyneth. That's Grandma's name. And in the olden days women used to change their names when they got married. Thompson to Green—it makes perfect sense. . . . Dani, Gwen is Grandma! She must be!"

Dani was silent, stunned. She stared at Gwen, asleep on her back. There was a smudge on her nose. Her hair was a mess. It didn't seem possible that this girl would grow up to be the formidable chief justice Gwyneth Green.

Sara laughed oddly. "Wow, Dani, can you believe it? I'm inside my own grandmother!" She paused. "Wouldn't you know it'd have to be somebody as pigheaded and bossy as Grandma?"

Dani said thoughtfully, "She's young now. Maybe she'll be different."

"You say she's going to do what she wants, no matter what *I* want. So, what else is new?"

Dani didn't say anything. She herself had always liked Mrs. G, but she knew Sara had often had arguments with her grandmother. She hadn't even wanted to live with her for the year that her parents were away. And now she actually had to *be* her. No wonder Sara sounded grim.

Sara suddenly said, "I wonder if Adam Duguay is here, too?"

"What?"

"He was holding on to my pendant when it broke, the way you said Gwen's dad was holding hers. And if *we* went back in time by breaking the pendant, then

Duguay is as likely to be here as we are. I'll bet he's inside Gwen's father."

"Wow," Dani said inadequately. She took a deep breath, shaking her head dazedly.

"Well, he's no worse off than me, if he is," Sara replied.

"I don't know about that," Dani said. "At least you know that we've time traveled. He can't have the slightest clue what's going on. If he is here, he must be feeling really—scared."

"That Greysuit? Come on."

They were both silent for a moment. Then Sara said, "Dani, what about getting back to our own time? I mean, things can't stay like this forever, can they?"

Until now, Dani had not thought of this. It had been enough to figure things out a step at a time, and to know that even if she might not have a body that people in this century could see or hear, at least Sara was with her. But now . . .

"I don't know what we can do," she said at last. "You're stuck inside Mrs. G, and she—"

"Let's keep calling her Gwen," Sara interrupted. "It's too weird, the other way."

"Well, then, Gwen's going to keep on doing what she usually does, unless we're wrong about the time-travel rules. That means *you* won't be able to do anything to get us back to our own time. If Mr. Duguay is here, he won't be able to do anything, either. And without a body, what can *I* do?"

"We'll find a way," Sara said determinedly. "We have to get born sometime, don't we? If time really has got its own rules, one of them's bound to be not to let people exist in two places at once. Eventually we'll all be back to normal."

But it would be a very long time before twelve-year-old Gwen would grow up enough to become a grand-mother to a baby called Sara, Dani thought. Fifty years, at least. It was a long time to be stuck in somebody else's body. And it might, she told herself gloomily, feel even longer when you had no body at all.

Chapter Eight

S OMETHING was happening.
Inside the warm darkness of her grandmother's body, Sara stirred uneasily. Stinging eyes opened to a green dimness. Knuckles assaulted those eyes. A hand, outflung, struck bark. It hurt. Gwen was awake.

Sara had hoped she would fall asleep when Gwen awoke, but unfortunately she didn't feel at all sleepy. It seemed likely that she was going to have to stay awake while Grandma's younger self went through the routine of her usual life. It wasn't a pleasant prospect. Her grandmother had already told her too much about her old-fashioned past for Sara to hope that the two of them would have any interests in common. And she knew she wouldn't enjoy even five minutes of tagging along, doing nothing herself while the body she was in did boring things. The thought of going through that kind of thing day after day for an unknowable period of time made her feel vaguely sick.

Except that it was Grandma's stomach that felt sick, not her own. How awful to share a stomach with her grandmother. With *Gwen*, Sara reminded herself, Gwen, not Grandma. It was interesting that Gwen's stomach felt sick because of thoughts that she, Sara, was having. Maybe she could influence Gwen's body in other ways, too. Maybe Dani was wrong, and she could actually make Gwen do things.

Suddenly Gwen sat up. Sara sat up, too. She felt herself doing it, and tried to stop, but it was useless. When

Gwen peered around the little hollow under the tree and saw nothing except branches and brown pine needles and soft moss and stone, Sara saw nothing but those things, too. Most particularly, she saw no signs of Dani. It didn't matter that her mind knew Dani would be right beside her, anxious and lonely and needing to be seen. Sara could not see her through Gwen's eyes, and they were the only eyes she had.

She tried to speak to Dani, but Gwen's lips stayed stubbornly closed. Then she tried forming words in her mind, but that was no good either. Either Dani couldn't hear Sara's attempts, or she was answering, but Sara couldn't hear her reply. Maybe she could use Gwen's ears for her own purposes only when the conscious Gwen was asleep. If so, as long as Gwen was awake, Sara was as isolated from her friend as if Dani were not there at all.

Great, Sara thought. I can't move when Gwen's asleep, and I can't communicate when she's awake. What a horrible situation.

Horrible, Gwen thought suddenly. Mom will be worried if I don't go back to the house, but if I go back, I'll have to see Dad. . . .

It was strange to hear somebody else thinking. In a way it felt as if she were thinking Gwen's thoughts herself. She didn't like that idea at all. I'm me, Sara Melody Green, she told herself fiercely; I'm just boarding for a while in my grandmother's body. I don't have to *be* her, just because I'm *in* her.

Gwen was uneasy. "Is somebody there?" she said suddenly.

Sara was still, struggling not to be uneasy herself. There had been nothing to hear out there. Gwen was imagining things.

Gwen scrambled forward on her knees, parted the

branches, peered out. Sara peered with her. A path, more trees, then bare boulders, prickly shrubs. Openness. Sara shivered. Gwen shivered, too.

"Nothing," she muttered. "I'm imagining things."

She looked at her watch. It was an old-fashioned thing with a big hand and a little hand, like one of Joshua's old clocks. Sara looked at it with Gwen. Seven o'clock, she told herself. Supper.

It was interesting to be able to tell time on an old-fashioned watch. It was interesting to be hungry with someone else's stomach.

Maybe this isn't going to be as boring as I thought, Sara told herself.

And then Gwen pushed her way out of her hidey-hole and stood up, and Sara wanted to scream.

They were virtually at the top of a high hill. The tree they had hidden under was the last on the slope. A vista as big as forever spread out from this rocky open hilltop, encompassing bare rocks and treetops, the roof of a house far below, the lake, and one end of a dock. And then there were more trees, more and more of them, green and black and green and black marching away from the lake into a mass of hills in the distance. The lake was mirror smooth and dark, shadowed by the cliff and the forest and the approach of sunset. A canoe was tied up to the dock, small as a toy. Gwen threw her head back and gulped in the cool wind. The sky overhead was pale blue and violet, and huge, huge.

Sara tried to close her eyes tight. Gwen shut hers, then rubbed them hard and determinedly opened them again. A bird took off from the lake, leaving a thin silver wake as it dragged its feet through the last stretch of water. Then it was up, its high, mournful cry piercing the sky. *Keerkeeee, keerkeee, kee, kee, kee.*

Gwen watched it. Sara trembled, but she watched it, too; she had to. "It's bad enough for you," Gwen muttered to the bird, "and you don't even nest here. But my loons . . ."

I don't like loons, Sara thought. If it hadn't been for loons, I wouldn't be here. I want to get off this hilltop. I want to get *inside*.

Mom will be worried, Gwen thought again.

She started down the path, heading for the big old house overlooking the lake, bounding down the path at a speed Sara would have admired in anyone else. It was odd how well she avoided tangles while still keeping her eyes down, dipping gracefully under overhanging bushes and leaping stones that jutted out of the mossy, needle-strewn earth. Her footing was solid and her balance secure. She must know this path very well indeed to take it so quickly, Sara thought. The speed was exhilarating. Sara could almost forget she was outside in this horrible place. It was almost fun.

Fun! Suddenly Sara was angry at herself. This was Grandma who ran like this, Grandma who would probably be reading law books all the time she wasn't being nice to her twin brothers or singing songs with her family around the keyboard or going out for dumb walks in the moonlight. And she would be making Sara do all those things with her. It would be worse, much worse, than the six months Sara had lived with her in Ottawa.

I've got to get away! Sara thought. I've got to get back home!

She looked up. The wooden steps to the big front porch were just ahead.

Home.

✦

88

Even with nothing to distract Gwen in the hollow of that tree, she had still looked right through Dani.

So I am invisible, Dani thought. *I* can see me, but no one else can, not even Sara.

No one could hear her, either. Out on the hilltop, Dani had yelled Sara's name as loudly as she could, but there had been no result. Despairingly, Dani had clamped her hand to Gwen's wrist, keeping it there all the time Gwen ran. The thin blond girl was too fast for Dani, especially going downhill. It was the way Sara would have run, and it made Dani scared. But she didn't dare let go of Gwen's wrist. She couldn't risk being left behind. There was a path to the house, so she wouldn't get lost; but what if Gwen and Sara got inside the house before Dani could get there, and the door was locked between them and her?

They were almost to the house now, running up some wooden steps that had been built over the big pink rocks. The house was huge—the biggest private dwelling Dani had ever seen. It had three wings: the large central one Gwen was making for now, a long and narrow addition at the western end, and the part at the back that Dani had been able to see from the hill above. Everything looked to be made of wood, some painted white, the rest a lovely natural silver grey. All the way around the front and continuing along the side overlooking the lake was a raised open section with thick poles holding up a roof. Anxious as she was, Dani marveled at this. A floor and a ceiling but no walls! Just fresh air to breathe and beautiful views to look at, with slatted wooden chairs to sit on and tables grouped invitingly all around.

And real books, Dani thought. Real books tossed casually on the tables. Dani had seen pictures of books in the televids, and she'd actually touched a book kept in a glass case in her school library. She knew how valuable they were. How could people just leave them outside, where the weather could get at them or somebody might steal them?

A woman came out of the front door as they headed across a narrow moss-covered flat toward the final staircase. "You're late," she said crossly to Gwen, her hands on her hips. "You know when I serve dinner. And I made steak, too, your favorite."

She was a tired-looking woman—in her thirties, Dani guessed. Her skin was almost as brown as Gwen's, and there were small darker spots of color speckling her nose and arms. She wore a sleeveless shirt and pale blue pants that were like the jeans Mrs. G had worn. Her hair was a lovely chestnut color, and made Dani think of horses.

"Hello," Dani said, not very hopefully.

"Your brothers are starving," the woman said. "Bugging me all afternoon for a lick of your birthday-cake icing. And now they'll have to wait till your dad comes back. Can't have birthday cake without the whole family here."

"Sorry, Mom," Gwen muttered. Dani could feel the tension in her. "Where'd Dad go?"

"He ate early, if you can call it eating. The amount he got down, it was more like something was eating him. Then out he went, not a word about where. What did you two get up to, there on the dock?"

"We were arguing," Gwen said uncomfortably.

"About the mill?" Gwen jerked her head in assent, her eyes on the ground. "Oh, Gwennie, I asked you to give it a while before you talked to your dad. It was why I told you about the mill first, while he was out fishing. I thought you'd handle it better, coming from me. You know Al's not good at telling people things when he's miserable—"

"Sure he's miserable, Mom. He's so miserable about selling this place he's going to let a sawmill come in and ruin it."

"We've had it on the market for two years. No one else has offered to buy it. Can you blame them? Great big lodge like this, and one of the nicest weekends we've had all summer, and not a single guest in sight."

"There are people coming in at the end of the week."

"Nine," Mrs. Thompson said. "And at package rates. We'll net enough to pay about two days' worth of the mortgage on this place."

"We've always got by before!"

"There wasn't a recession on before. Nobody's got money to spend on ordinary vacations, not anymore. People with money go to places like Tahiti."

Gwen aimed a resentful kick at the bottom step, then climbed slowly to the porch. Dani looked from one of them to the other. How could she see them both so clearly when to them she might not have been there at all?

"I've lived here all my life," Gwen mumbled thickly into her collar. "It isn't fair."

"Life isn't fair," her mother said. She reached out a hand appealingly, trying to smile. "But at least we'll have some money after this. You can have new clothes, go to college when you're old enough. . . ."

Gwen looked up, but ignored the extended hand. "I don't care about that."

Mrs. Thompson's hand dropped to her side. Dani saw her lips thin. Her blue eyes scanned Gwen's face, then dropped to her neck. "Where's your pendant?" she said suddenly.

Dani could feel Gwen's arm begin to shake. "Dad's got it."

91

"Why?"

"It—broke."

Her mother looked horrified. Her hands rose to her face, one on either cheek. "Broke? Not the crystal part? Oh, Gwennie, not the crystal! It was one of a kind—irreplaceable—"

"The chain, not the crystal."

"Thank God." She shook her head, relieved, then frowned. "The day you got it, for heaven's sake. How'd it happen?"

"I'm hungry," Gwen said abruptly.

For a long moment her mother only looked at her. "I told your dad how you mooned after that pendant the last time we were in Toronto. First thing Al did when we decided to accept the mill's offer was to phone that store. The pendant was still there. He had it sent."

"Trying to buy me off," Gwen said bitterly.

"Trying to give you something you loved," Mrs. Thompson corrected her.

"I'd rather have the land. I told Dad so. Let him take the pendant back to the store. I don't want it."

The woman took a deep breath. "They wouldn't likely take it back. And your dad paid for it on the charge card. Pretty much took our credit to the limit. There's not money to pay for it without the mill deal going through."

"So now it's my fault? Because Dad got me that pendant, the deal has to go through?"

Dani didn't know which of them she felt sorrier for. With a visible attempt at calm, Gwen's mother said, "Now, get this in your head, Gwen. The deal will go through anyway. We've already signed the contract. We're out of here at the end of the summer."

Gwen was shaking all over now. She pushed past her mother into the house. Then, with Dani invisible by her

92

side, she marched across the wide front room to the place where it opened into two corridors, meeting each other at right angles. "Where are you going?" Mrs. Thompson called from just inside the front door.

"To my room. I suppose it *is* still mine, isn't it? Till the end of the summer?"

"I thought you were hungry!"

"Not anymore."

Dani took her hand from Gwen's wrist as the blond girl turned to the right. Sara was inside Gwen, but as long as Gwen was awake, Dani couldn't reach her. Staying in Gwen's room doing nothing until Gwen slept wouldn't be much use. She watched Gwen heading down a long, dim passage full of doors with numbers on them. She had never seen anyone's back so erect.

"You think you're the only one who cares," Gwen's mother called after her. "That's right, go off and chew on your selfishness. But it's a mean meal for a birthday dinner!"

Wordlessly, Gwen opened a door to her left. A second later, she was out of sight, the door slamming behind her. Mrs. Thompson stood, her shoulders slumping.

"Mom?" called a young voice from behind a closed door ahead and to Dani's left. "Hey, Mom, we gonna eat soon? Billie and me are starving."

"Coming, Roy." She straightened, forced a smile on her face, and made her way to the heavy, swinging door that led to the adjoining room. Her path took her right by Dani, scarcely an arm's length between them.

"Hello," Dani said loudly. "My name is Danielle Fowler. I'm glad to—"

"Now, don't you two start on that steak till I've cut it up for you," Mrs. Thompson said, opening the door.

I'm not here for *anyone* in this place, Dani thought.

93

She followed Mrs. Thompson just closely enough to see that behind the door was a large dining table, and two identical little blond-headed kids sitting impatiently waiting. The door swung shut. Dani just stood there. For a while she kept still. It wasn't going to be that bad, being a ghost. She could move around by herself, something Sara couldn't do. She could see and hear everything that was going on. She could . . .

She hated it.

"We've got to get back to our own time," she muttered. "We've just got to."

A short while passed. Dani took a deep breath. There was no use her just standing here. She and Sara were stuck here for a while. She should find out what she could about the place.

She looked around her. The room was big and shabby and comfortable, lined with windows. There were extra-wide chairs and footstools and paintings on the walls and shelves simply crammed with books, but the most important thing about the room was its spaciousness. You could walk ten steps at least in any direction, Dani thought, ten steps without bumping into anything.

I'm going to walk, she decided.

Even on her own, it didn't feel like normal walking. She tried to figure out what was different about it. "I can feel the floor," she told herself. "But it—sort of—doesn't feel me."

Near Gwen's bedroom corridor there was a whole collection of framed homemade pictures. They drew her, somehow. They were brightly colored and immature, except that here and there the trees were right, the full moon was right, the birds were right, the rabbits running in the meadow were right. Dani knew they were right, even though she had seen such things mostly only in televids before. Obviously someone here had seen them alive.

Slowly she moved along the row of pictures. They turned the corner into the corridor, and Dani followed them. Just beside a door marked with a big number 1, the pictures stopped. There, in the dim light of a far-off electric bulb, was the picture of a horse.

Dani stood stock-still in front of it. It was a big grey stallion, one hoof raised, its head lowered a little as if it were thinking about cropping the grass at its feet. But it had wicked eyes, and its ears were pricked up; this horse was doing nothing as placid as grazing. The picture had been lovingly drawn and carefully colored, a long time taken over it. *My Uncle's Horse, Thunder* was the title printed in childish letters under the picture, and in smaller letters, as if the painter were determined to show which was more important: "by Gwennie Thompson, age 10."

Gwen's uncle has a horse, Dani thought dazedly. Gwen gets to see it sometimes.

And for the first time since arriving in the past, Dani found she was not even trying to think of a way to get home.

Chapter Nine

THERE was an animal on Gwen's bed.
Sara barely had time to observe the big, floppy
black ears and the lolling pink tongue before Gwen had
thrown herself on the beast, clutching it to her like a
lifeline. "Oh, Shags, Shags boy, what am I going to do?
I can't bear leaving here!"

The dog's pink tongue rasped on Gwen's arm. Sara
shivered. She had never been so close to a dog in her
life. Gwen shivered, too. The dog stirred uneasily, wrig-
gling away from Gwen's grasp and leaping off the bed.
It made purposefully for the farthest corner, then turned,
squeezing its body into as small a ball as possible and
facing Gwen with a wild-eyed stare.

Gwen frowned. "What's the matter, Shags? You look
scared."

She got off the bed as if to go to it. *Stop!* Sara willed
her. The dog growled, its ears flat to its head. Gwen
stopped.

"What on earth? Shags!" The dog's low growling
stopped. It panted hard. Gwen's brow furrowed. "Was I
holding you too hard? Was that it? Or did I wake you
in the middle of a bad dream?"

Still the dog panted. "You're hot. Maybe you need a
drink? Okay. I'll let you out." She opened the door, and,
with a scrabbling of claws, Shags was gone.

"Now what was that all about?" Gwen muttered. She
closed the door again and threw herself back on her bed,
staring unhappily at the ceiling. Her stomach growled.

Sara could understand Gwen losing her temper. She could even understand Gwen running away when she was mad and yelling at the wrong person if that person happened to get in the way. It was the sort of thing Sara might have done herself. But *Grandma* didn't do things like that. Grandma always got mad coolly and calmly, and she aimed her anger at the person who deserved it, not at somebody like that Mrs. Thompson, who had gone out of her way to make a nice birthday supper that now Gwen refused to eat.

Sara had heard of steak, even though in her time only Greysuits could afford to buy it. Mrs. Thompson didn't look as if she could afford it, but she had bought it for Gwen. Imagine turning down something that expensive to lie on your bed and sulk! Sara thought disapprovingly.

Gwen bit her lip. Mom with her ten-cents-off coupons and tight budget. And the mill money wouldn't have come through yet. Mom would have scrimped for weeks to make Gwen's favorite meal.

Her father wasn't even in the house, Sara told herself. Gwen was being pigheaded for nothing.

Gwen got to her feet. She opened her bedroom door and marched down the long hall to the big front room, then opened the swinging door to the dining room. Her mother looked up. "Any steak left, Mom?"

"Sit down," her mother said, not smiling, but with a look in her eyes that made up for it.

Gwen nodded and sat. She said something nice to one of her brothers. She helped the other one cut up his baked potato. "Maybe we can all play Scrabble after supper," she said.

Back to normal, Sara thought. The next thing you knew, Gwen would be volunteering to practice the keyboard or getting out that dumb old telescope Grandma had talked about to look at the stars.

✧

Dani tried to enjoy feeling light. At least her invisible muscles were loose and flexible. It wasn't important if the floor didn't seem to feel her weight. She could still do things.

She went to the outside door, placing her hand carefully on the knob. She could feel it perfectly well. She could see her hand on the knob, too, just as she could see her whole body. But when she tried turning the knob, it was like trying to turn air. Nothing happened.

"That's just great," she said aloud.

It made sense, though. People from the future couldn't be allowed to do anything to change history. What if someone came along right now and saw a doorknob turning apparently by itself and then the door opening all on its own without any visible reason? What if that scared the person so much he or she had a heart attack and died? That would change history, all right.

But that means I'm stuck here, Dani thought. I can't go outside without someone opening the door for me.

An animal bounded noisily into the room. She turned, staring at it interestedly. It was a dog, big and shiny-black and cuddly, and Dani loved it at once. "Hi, there," she said softly to it, even though the dog wouldn't hear her. But it skidded to a stop, its ears back. It gave a tiny whimper. Then, suddenly, it skittered over to the swinging door to the dining room, butted its big head against it, and disappeared inside.

Dani felt lonely again. She wanted Sara, but Sara was behind Gwen's bedroom door, completely out of reach. Even the dog had run away. I never had a pet, she thought. Gwen's so lucky. Her own dog, as well as an uncle with a horse.

Did Gwen's uncle live nearby? Dani stirred restlessly, then went over to the nearest window. It was dusk, the trees and rocks almost black with the approach of night. But Dani could just see the lake with its dock sticking out and a little house near the landward end of the dock. She strained to see farther. She had been too confused to pay attention to her surroundings when she'd been on the dock earlier. Now she wished she'd noticed more. That little house down by the water couldn't be Gwen's uncle's place, could it? Not likely. His place had a meadow, with a plank fence for the horse.

She tried the view from another window, but it told her no more. The buzz of conversation in the dining room made her lonelier than ever. Her lightness and freedom didn't count for anything at all if she couldn't go anywhere except within this room. Frustrated, she leaned her forehead against the wall. A real ghost would just walk straight through the walls, she thought. But she wasn't a real ghost. She was just somebody time had made invisible.

"A time ghost," she said aloud, to hear the sound of her own voice.

She was perfectly solid, of course, just invisible. She couldn't walk through a wall.

But she hadn't tried. And Sara would ask her what she'd done all evening, when they could talk again.

She stepped back from the wall, faced it, closed her eyes, and determinedly walked forward. Two steps, three, four. She opened her eyes.

She was outside.

I can walk through walls, she thought, and shivered. It was a thought as horrible as it was wonderful.

She stood on the steps, staring down the path to the lake. Night was falling fast. She had better hurry if she was going to see anything tonight. She started down, slowly at first, then running, jumping with both feet onto the pink rock and churning on down the path. It came out at the edge of the lake and led right onto the dock. The little house was beside the path a short distance off, sticking out into the water on what looked like wooden stilts. Dani made her way to it along the shore of the lake. A door in the back stood open. In the gloom she could make out two canoes floating in the water that filled the house from its open door on the other side.

"A house for boats," Dani murmured, shaking her head in amazement. She thought of the blockbuilding in Ottawa where she and Josh lived with their parents. This boathouse was bigger than her own and Josh's rooms put together. Josh wouldn't know what to say if he saw this.

Dani wished Josh *could* see it. But he was at the North Pole, in another century. He hadn't been born yet. *She* hadn't been born. It was a disturbing thought.

There was a wide space left in the middle of the boathouse. Other boats must be kept here ordinarily, Dani thought. Maybe Gwen's dad was out in one right now. She went back to the dock. A canoe was moored at the far end, and an old-fashioned rowboat closer to shore. They were the right size to fit into the empty place in the boathouse. That meant Gwen's dad hadn't gone out in a boat after all. She wondered where he was.

"And that Greysuit, too," she said aloud. Was he inside Gwen's dad or wasn't he? What should she do about it if he was? What *could* she do?

She sat on the end of the dock, her legs dangling, her arms hugging her chest. What now? What?

It was like all those times before she'd known Sara, trying to figure out what to do, and getting nowhere.

✧

They had the birthday cake at the twins' bedtime, even though Mr. Thompson wasn't there. Afterward, despite all Sara's protests, Gwen went outside. She stood on the veranda staring out, Sara trying uselessly not to stare with her, while behind them came the quiet voice of Mrs. Thompson reading a bedtime story.

The moon was a gleaming sickle hanging in the sky. Sara had never seen a sky like that in all her life. It was the deep violet blue of the velvet box Grandma had given her, but glittering with stars. The trees sighed, leaning over the silver lake. Water lapped the shore and gurgled under the dock, gentle as a lullaby. A bird called softly, like weird laughter far off.

Hooo hooooooooooo, hoo-hoo-hoooo.

My loons, Gwen thought.

Before Sara knew what was happening, Gwen was racing down the path. Where was she going, out here in the dark? A cool breeze fingered Gwen's hair. Sara remembered the last time her hair had felt like that, one long red curl lifting and dancing while she had walked with Dani and Grandma toward an eelgrass-filled sea.

Still Gwen ran. When the moon filled the open places Sara cringed, but in the shadows it was like flying. Again the loons called. *Hooo hooooooooooo, hoo-hoo-hoooo.*

Lovely. So lovely. Even Sara could hear that it was.

The jagged silver moonlight flashed again. They were out in the open. There was no cover now, there were no trees to hide under, nothing but an infinity of sky. The glinting lake caught the light and threw it at Sara. She hated it, hated the pitiless sky, hated the tranquillity and the cool freshness of the air. Most of all she hated Gwen for making her come out here. Ordinary people did ordinary things like going to bed and reading bedtime stories. But not Gwen. Not Grandma.

Gwen reached the dock, thudded to the end, and stopped.

The loons were silent.

"Don't go," Gwen begged urgently. "Please don't go. You've got all summer."

She sat down on the end of the dock. Silence descended on the lake. The water was still, the moon swimming in it. Space was everywhere. Sara could scarcely bear it.

Go inside, Sara commanded Gwen despairingly. *Grandma, please, go inside.*

But still Gwen sat at the end of the dock and waited.

✧

"Sara," Dani said. "Sara, can you hear me?"

The moon was lost behind the hill, and the air cooler. Gwen lay still, curled up on the end of the dock, breathing evenly in the faint, glittery starlight.

"Dani! You're here! Oh, thank goodness! I was afraid you'd be stuck up in the lodge or something. Did you come out with us? Have you been here all along? I thought I'd go crazy — the quiet, and all that watching and watching, and being all alone with her. . . ."

"*I* was with you," Dani said. It wasn't Sara's fault she hadn't known.

"At first I hoped she'd go inside. But oh no. Then I hoped she would fall asleep, but it's been *hours*."

"Poor Sara," Dani said.

"It must have been pretty bad for you, too," Sara said after a minute. "I couldn't see you, Dani. Not once since we got here. I tried and tried, but I couldn't. Did you

103

try to talk to me? I couldn't hear you if you did. Has it been awful?"

Yes, it had been awful. Dani took a breath. "I can walk through walls."

"Really? Lucky! What does it feel like?"

Dani thought of trying to explain. Then she shrugged. "What does it feel like to be inside somebody else?"

"Weird. Interesting, sometimes. But horrible, too. I miss being me, Dani. I miss *doing* things—doing them for myself, I mean. I hate doing what somebody else wants all the time. I can't even close my eyes when Gwen's got hers open. And I hate it out here. It's so — *big*."

"It's beautiful, though."

"But who wants to sit outside in the middle of the night waiting for a couple of stupid birds to call to each other? Anybody else would be in bed at two in the morning—or three, or whatever it is now. Two was the last time Gwen looked at her watch."

"I saw her," Dani said. "It was when that car drove up to the lodge."

"Gwen thought it was her dad coming back."

"You can hear her thoughts, then?"

"Unless I tune them out," Sara said grimly. "It's like having a radio on all the time. She doesn't think the way I do, Dani. She likes her brothers. She likes emptiness and quiet. She likes this place. And she *loves* those darn loons."

"I know," Dani said. "She told us on the icebreaker, when she was Mrs. G, remember?"

"She gets angrier than I would have guessed," Sara went on after a moment. "It's about the only thing we have in common."

"She runs like you," Dani pointed out. "Without having to think, I mean. . . . Sara, if you hear her thoughts, can she hear yours?"

"Sometimes I think so. But I tried to get her to go inside, earlier, and she didn't. She couldn't have heard me thinking then."

"I'm not sure you should try to get her to do what you want," Dani said, thinking about time rules and changing history.

"Not much point," Sara agreed bitterly. "Grandma always does what *she* wants."

"I wonder why Gwen's dad was out so late?" Dani muttered after a moment.

"Maybe it was something to do with that Greysuit."

"How could it be?"

"Well, if he really is inside Gwen's dad—" She broke off, then added thoughtfully, "You know, Dani, I think we should try to find that out. Adam Duguay is a grown-up. If he *is* here, maybe he'll have some ideas how the three of us can get home. We should go up to the house while Mr. Thompson's asleep and find out."

"We? You mean me, don't you? I mean, *you* won't be able to go anywhere until Gwen wakes up. And you couldn't *say* anything to Mr. Duguay unless she was asleep."

There was a moment's disconcerted silence. Then Sara said, "I guess you're right, Dani. You're on your own in this one."

"What should I say to him?"

"Start off like this," Sara said. " 'Mr. Duguay, sir, are you inside Al Thompson?' " She giggled. "And then you should say, 'We'll get you out if you promise not to drill for oil in the Arctic.' "

"But we can't *get* him out!" Dani protested.

"Honestly, Dani, can't you tell when I'm joking? Just explain what's happened, and see what he says."

"I'll have to be careful not to wake up Gwen's mother," Dani said, after a moment. "She'll be there, too."

"Don't worry about that," Sara said. "Nobody who belongs in this time can hear you."

"But she can hear *his* voice," Dani said. "If Duguay really is there, he'll have to talk to me, and to do that—"

"Warn him to keep his voice down, then."

Sara sounded impatient. Dani knew she wished she could be the one to go up there and talk to Mr. Duguay. That would have been fine with Dani. She didn't want to go by herself into that darkened lodge. But if Mr. Duguay really was inside Al Thompson, he must be having a pretty awful time of it. He would have had no one to explain to him about time travel and the North Pole. And there was Mr. Thompson to worry about. Dani kept remembering how Gwen's mother had described the way Mr. Thompson had eaten at dinner. *More like something was eating him.* And he'd gone away somewhere and hadn't come back until after two. Had Mr. Duguay had something to do with that? What if Al Thompson had heard Duguay thinking, and it had been that that had sent him out driving in the night?

"Okay, I'll try it," Dani said. She got to her feet, looking down at Gwen, sleeping so peacefully in the dark. For a long moment she hesitated.

"Are you still there?" Sara's voice was anxious.

"I'm just going. You'll be all right?"

"Her eyes are closed," Sara muttered. "I don't have to see."

"I'll be back soon."

"Yes. Please." And almost as an afterthought: "Good luck."

Dani sighed. "I hope I don't need it," she said.

Chapter Ten

THERE were no lights on in the lodge. Dani hesitated nervously on the veranda, then closed her eyes and walked toward the nearest wall. She took five or six steps. With each one she felt the usual uncomfortable sensation of touching the floor without making any impression on it. Nothing changed as she went forward. Was she through the wall or not? She opened her eyes. It was even darker than before.

I must be inside, she told herself. It's always darker inside than out.

The big room seemed very black. Dani didn't like it. But Sara was all alone down there on the dock, outside and hating it.

It won't matter if I do bump into something, Dani told herself; I'll just go through it, the way I went through the wall.

The important thing was to hurry. Where did Gwen's parents sleep? Down the same corridor as Gwen, probably. She fumbled forward, arms stretched out like a sleepwalker's, eyes wide.

Slowly the darkness took form. Furniture was a thicker blackness; the light-colored walls, reflecting starlight from the open windows, a thinner one. Dani fumbled her way across the room. Gwen's bedroom corridor had no windows, she remembered. It would be darker than the big main room. Yes. There. She turned right, straining to see. She didn't want to walk through any walls by mistake. It would be too easy to get lost.

She counted her steps, walking down the corridor. When she got to six, she paused. She must be well beyond that painting of Thunder now. Where might the Thompsons' bedroom be? Maybe Gwen's father would be snoring. She listened hard. Nothing. Seven, eight, nine, ten . . . It was hard to believe any place could be this dark. If she got to the end of the corridor, she would have to start checking every bedroom. Fifteen, sixteen . . . She stopped. There was a noise just ahead and to her left, a snuffling, animal-like sound, followed by a low growl.

The dog! It must be in one of the bedrooms. And somehow it sensed that Dani was out here. She had read that dogs could be sensitive to ghosts.

The dog barked.

It was a loud, urgent sound. Dani stood frozen, not knowing what to do. The dog kept barking. One of the twins began to cry. It sounded as if the dog was in the room with him.

"What's the matter with Shags?"

It was Mrs. Thompson's voice, from farther down the hall. Dani grimaced. If Shags didn't wake Al Thompson, Mrs. Thompson would be bound to. And then, even if Adam Duguay was there, he wouldn't be able to talk to Dani. He wouldn't even hear her. Dani hesitated. Maybe she should just turn around and go.

"Al, did you shut Shags up in the boys' room?" No answer. "He must want to go out, to bark like that. Al?" Still no answer. "Oh, for heaven's sake!"

There was a sound like two bare feet slapping on the floor. On the point of fleeing, Dani changed her mind. After all, she told herself, I am invisible. To people, anyway.

A door opened, and the darkness in the corridor thinned a little. A muttering silhouette emerged. Dani's heart thudded. She made a bolt for the open door, passing Mrs. Thompson just as the woman reached the room where the dog was barking frenziedly.

"All right, you dumb dog, all right!" Mrs. Thompson said, opening the door and grabbing at Shags as he bounded out. She sounded very annoyed. Dani didn't wait to see more. She scurried into the Thompsons' bedroom. In the other room, Gwen's mother said, "Go back to sleep, Billie. You don't need to cry because a stupid dog barks. You, too, Roy. What's going on with everyone tonight?" Shags kept right on barking.

It was not nearly as dark in the Thompsons' bedroom as in the hall, because there were two big windows letting in the starlight. The bed was between the windows, a dark lump of a head on one of the pillows. Al Thompson was breathing like one deeply asleep. Trembling, Dani went over to him. The dog's barking continued, but the sounds were getting more distant. Gwen's mother must be taking him outside. Good.

"Mr. Duguay," Dani said quietly, nervously. "Mr. Duguay, are you there?"

"Thank God," said Adam Duguay through Al Thompson's mouth. "What — who — is there really someone there who knows me? Who are you? Why can't I see you?"

Dani shuddered with relief. "It's me, Danielle Fowler. Sara Green's friend. From the puffhover. You can't see me because— *he's* got his eyes closed. He's asleep."

There was a pause. "He. What do you mean, 'he'?"

"Al Thompson. Gwen's father. You're — well, you're inside him."

111

"Inside—!" There was a long pause. Then, suspiciously, "What did you say your name was?"

"Dani. Don't you remember me? You held my arm on the *Seabeater*, and you asked me if it mattered to the boys' experiment if they were right over the North Pole —you know, Josh and Karl?—Karl is Mrs. G's grandson, I mean, Counselor Green's—and I said it did matter, so we went to tell them they were in the wrong place and Mrs. G heard a loon and—"

"You seem to know a great deal about those events, at least. I find it hard to understand how—if you weren't . . ." His voice trailed off. He began again almost at once, though. "This last while I've been seeing places that aren't anything like the North Pole. And cars and boats and toilets and things that are straight out of the history vids. And I keep trying to do things, only it feels as if somebody else is in charge of my body. Sometimes I think I've been asleep for days, and others, well, I wonder if I might be—ill."

"Oh, Mr. Duguay, it's not that. It's because you've time traveled."

"Time traveled! You're joking. People can't—"

"They can. We did. It was Josh who figured it out. He knew that all the time zones in the world meet at the North Pole, so that it's really all times at once there. He thought that meant the North Pole might be kind of like a doorway through time." She was gabbling, she knew, but she had to make him understand. "I overheard Josh tell Karl about it, so when you and Sara broke her chain and the three of us came here, I knew what had happened. I mean, at first I thought I was dreaming, but—"

"I'm dreaming this conversation right now, I think."

"It's not a dream. Really. You *must* know that, Mr. Duguay. It's too real to be a dream."

"I'd rather think it was a dream than — " Duguay began.

"If you're dreaming it, so am I. Listen. The lake's got a dock, and a boathouse, and canoes and trees, and the house is built on pink rocks and it's got three wings and — "

"Two of us with the same dream," Duguay said wryly. "It does sound unlikely."

"It's all real. You're seeing it with Al Thompson's eyes. You *are* inside him, Mr. Duguay. Think about it. When Mr. Thompson is awake you must wonder why you're suddenly the owner of this lodge, and are poor, and are selling the lodge to a sawmill, and have three kids. Gwen's one of them. She's — "

"You're talking too fast," Duguay complained. "I can't listen to you and think at the same time."

Dani was silent.

"Gwen. The blond girl. What were you going to tell me about her?"

Dani decided not to explain that Gwen was really Sara's grandmother. He was being slow enough accepting things as it was. "Sara is inside Gwen," Dani said carefully, "the same way you're inside Gwen's father. It was because you and Sara broke her chain the same way Gwen and her dad broke— "

"And you?" Calmly, almost with amusement. "What other person are you inside?"

"You don't believe me, do you?" Duguay said nothing. After a moment Dani answered his question. "I'm not inside anybody. I'm kind of a time ghost. Nobody here can see me or hear me. Only Sara can hear me, and now you. And she can only do it when Gwen's asleep."

113

"Just a minute. Stop. I have to think."

They were both silent. In the distance Mrs. Thompson could be heard yelling exasperatedly at Shags, who was still barking.

Duguay said slowly, "I do remember breaking a chain. It had a crystal pendant attached. A loon. Counselor Green wanted me to see what they looked like. And then something odd happened. . . ."

"You and Sara were exactly over the North Pole when you broke her chain. That was kind of like a key, unlocking the time door. It opened, and you and Sara went through it to the time Gwen and her father broke their chain." There was no need to tell him the chains were one and the same. "I came along because I had my hand on Sara's arm. And you became Gwen's father and Sara became Gwen, and I—"

"Why become other people at all? Why not just stay ourselves?"

"We think it's a rule of time travel, to keep people from doing anything that might change the course of history. If you're in somebody else's body—somebody who actually lived here—or if you've got no body at all, then you can't do anything that would change the past. That means—"

"Yes. Yes, I see. Let me think."

Dani shut up, her hands clenching and unclenching. A minute passed. Mrs. Thompson had stopped yelling.

Duguay said, "Is that woman coming back?"

"Yes. Soon. We've got to hurry. She can't see or hear me, but you use Al's voice, so she'll hear you. Do you believe me at all, Mr. Duguay? Even just a little?"

When Duguay spoke again there was a strange note, almost of appeal, in his voice. "It's a crazy notion, but it would explain why my body isn't being very—obedient."

"It's Al Thompson's body that isn't being obedient. I don't think—oh, Mr. Duguay, *don't* try to make him do things. It might change history."

"Do you have any theories," he asked politely, but with the appeal still in his voice, "about how people might get back to a place like the *Seabeater* in the year 2044?"

"No," Dani admitted. "We hoped you would think of something."

There was another pause. "It's a bit of a disadvantage, I'd say, for us not to be at the North Pole now. Because it's only at the two Poles that the world's time zones all meet. If young Josh's theories are correct—"

A door slammed. Dani jumped. "Oh! She's coming!"

"—then the two Poles will be the only places in the world where time doors might actually be. And—just supposing all this is true, well, then, no time door, no time travel."

"You mean, we'd have to be at the North Pole to get back to our own time?" Dani choked out. She felt the room sliding away from her. "But we can't—I mean, how could we? Even in 2044 the North Pole is hard to get to."

"True. And with the primitive technology I've seen in this godforsaken place, I don't—"

He broke off. There were footsteps outside. Dani watched the open doorway, feeling too drained to move. Mrs. Thompson came in, then tried to shut the door gently, but it slipped from her fingers and clicked.

Al Thompson gave a snort and sat bolt upright. "That you, Dorrie?"

"Sorry I woke you. Though an earthquake couldn't have done it ten minutes ago."

"What's up?"

"Stupid dog smelled a fox or something," Gwen's mother said. "Wouldn't shut up. I had to tie him up outside, finally. Are you all right, Al? You were sleeping like the dead."

"I was tired, Dorrie. God, but I was tired."

"Where were you tonight? It was after one when I went to sleep, and you still weren't home. Where were you?"

"I don't know. Honestly, Dorrie. I was out there, driving the damned car halfway to Toronto, and I don't know how I got there, or why."

Even immersed in her own despair, Dani could hear the fear in his voice. Obviously, so could Dorrie. Her hand went to the light switch, turned it on. She smoothed her hair, tried to smile. "Okay, how many drinks did you have?"

"None. Nothing. I was just—there. It was like somebody else was driving, and I was the passenger." His voice was shaking.

Dorrie Thompson got into bed, then put her arms around her husband. "You were upset. Selling to the mill —Gwen being so mad—you've been under a lot of strain lately. It's okay, Al. Hush, now. It's okay."

"I don't know about the mill, Dorrie. I just don't know anymore."

"You've signed the contract."

"I know. And we have to have the money. But this house—the lake—maybe Gwennie's right that I've done a terrible thing—I just don't know. . . ."

He was crying. Dani had never seen a grown-up cry before. She couldn't watch anymore. It was too horrible.

She turned her back and made for the outside wall. Far away up the hill, Shags was howling. It was still deep night outside. Hardly any time at all had passed.

116

No time door. No way back.

She went down to the dock, down to Sara. Behind her, the lighted windows stared into the darkness, like two square eyes.

❖

"I don't believe it," Sara said emphatically, when Dani had told her everything. "There's no way we're stuck here forever. If necessary, Duguay will just have to force Gwen's dad to use some of the money from the mill to go on an expedition to the North Pole."

"Duguay shouldn't try to make Mr. Thompson do something he wouldn't ordinarily do. Look what happened tonight. The poor man ended up halfway to Toronto and thought he was going crazy. If it happens again, he might really go out of his mind. Even if it weren't a rotten thing to do to him, it would change history for sure. We can't do that."

"Who says? Just you, Dani. It's just one of your *ideas* that says time won't allow you to change history."

Dani was silent, trying to hide her hurt. Just one of her "ideas." And she was sure she was right, she was absolutely sure.

Sara was going on. "The hardest thing isn't going to be getting back to the North Pole. What I'm worried about is how we're going to unlock the time door once we get there." Silence. "Are you still here, Dani?" There was a sudden uncertainty in Sara's voice.

Dani took a deep breath. Sara was Sara. Her best friend. "Yes, I'm here."

"It's got to be something to do with that pendant," Sara said, confident again. "Breaking it brought us here. Maybe fixing it would get us back."

"I don't know," Dani said slowly. "It sounds too easy, somehow."

"It can't hurt to try."

"Gwen's dad has the pendant," Dani said. "He's too mad at her to get it fixed."

"I know. We'd have to make him fix it."

There she goes again, Dani thought. Making, forcing. But there was no point getting into an argument about it. "If you did that," Dani said carefully, "wouldn't you have to be right at the North Pole while you got the pendant's chain fixed?"

"I don't see why."

"Because if it needed *both* the North Pole *and* the breaking to bring us here, it'd need *both* the North Pole *and* the fixing to take us back."

Sara was silent. Then, reluctantly, she said, "I suppose that does make sense."

"And you'd need a jeweler to fix the thing," Dani persisted. "A jeweler at the North Pole."

"We could make Gwen's dad hire one to come with us." She paused, but Dani didn't reply. "I guess that's pretty complicated, isn't it? There must be an easier way."

"Yes," Dani said.

"Okay, what if we fix the chain first, and then break it again at the North Pole?"

"*Break* it to get home? But didn't you just say it was *fixing* the chain that would—?"

"That was one idea. This is another. Listen, Dani." She was getting excited now. "In 2044 we did exactly what Gwen and her father did, and it brought us back to their time. So if we repeated the whole thing again—I mean, if we got Gwen and her dad to go up to the North Pole and do *now* what we did in 2044—I mean, break the thing—hey, why wouldn't it take us home again?"

Dani thought about it. It sounded logical. But the

whole plan depended on the North Pole. Mrs. G had said she'd never been to the Arctic when she was young. If they made Gwen, Mrs. G's younger self, go there now, that would change history. "I don't know," she said dubiously.

"What don't you know?" Sara said impatiently, almost angrily.

Dani couldn't think what to say. Sara had already made fun of her ideas about time rules. "It just doesn't sound right," she mumbled.

"Are you doing this on purpose?" Sara asked suddenly.

"What do you mean?"

"Making up reasons why everything I say won't work?"

"No," Dani said. "No, I'm not." Sara was so angry! "I thought—I thought we were trying to figure things out together," she whispered a little tearfully.

Sara sighed impatiently. "Oh, for heaven's sake, don't cry."

"I'm not."

"You are." Her voice softened. "Dani, I'm sorry. Really. I didn't mean—"

Dani scrubbed at her eyes, trying not to sniff. "It's okay. Forget it."

"It's just that you don't usually—"

"Have ideas?" Dani said, raising her chin.

"No. I mean—your ideas are usually—"

"More like yours?"

There was a long silence. Then Sara said, slowly and with difficulty, "I guess, yes, that was what I meant. Oh, Dani, try to understand. I *hate* being inside somebody else. I *hate* it that you're the one who can move around and do things and talk to people and I can't. When Gwen's awake, I've got to do what she does, and when

119

she's asleep, the only thing I can do is think. *You* can do everything you want, and think as well. And I've been trying so hard to come up with ways to get home, and you've dug holes in every one of them. It makes me feel so *useless.* I know that's not why you're doing it, and I'm sorry I've been mean. But, Dani, we've got—*got*—to get back to our own bodies!"

Dani felt a lot better. She understood. "I know we have to get back. It's okay. Really."

"And anything that'll get us there—any idea at all— we have to think about."

"Yes," Dani said. But in her heart she wasn't so sure.

Chapter Eleven

THE breeze shifted. It had been light enough to see for more than an hour, but only now did dawn rim the canopy of trees greening the eastern horizon. Gwen slept on her back, her mouth open, but Sara was silent. For a long time she and Dani had had nothing to say.

Dani had spent the time watching the sky change. From starry black it had turned inky, then grey. Now it was the gentlest, softest rose she had ever seen. Clouds blossomed above the trees on the other side of the lake. Living green trees, pink sky, alabaster clouds, the blue of sun-warmed water . . . She had never thought to see colors like these, not in all her life.

"I'm going to try to wake Gwen up, Dani."

Dani turned to her, startled. "Why? If you do, we won't be able to talk."

"Just to see if I can. And we're not doing much talking now, anyway."

Dani couldn't stop herself. "Don't wake her, Sara. The day will be long enough."

Once Gwen was awake, Dani wouldn't be real to anyone. She wouldn't matter to anyone. Except that dog, Dani thought. And he had run the other way.

"Gwen might go inside if I wake her up," Sara said after a moment. When Dani didn't reply she added, "Maybe I'll be able to make Gwen have a sleep this afternoon. That way you and I could talk before tonight."

Waking Gwen up, sending her back to sleep . . . "Sara, please don't try to make Gwen do things. What if—?"

"— it changes history?" Sara finished for her. "How can waking up or having a nap change history?"

"Maybe by having a nap she'll miss doing something important she really *did* do when you weren't here to make her sleep."

"All right, all right." Morosely Sara added, "But it would have made a nice change to be the one to order Grandma around, instead of being on the receiving end all the time."

Footsteps crunched on pebbly stone. Dani looked up. "What's happening?" Sara asked.

"It's your — I mean, Gwen's — dad," she said. Al Thompson was trudging down the path from the lodge. "He's coming here. You'd better stop talking, Sara. He'll be able to hear you."

"He'll just think Gwen's talking in her sleep," Sara said indifferently.

Out on the lake, a bird called. It was the same call as the night before, only closer this time. Dani strained her eyes to catch a glimpse of this loon that Gwen loved so much, but could see only a line of distant splashes. In a moment the first birdcall was answered down the lake by another.

"Oh, Gwennie!" Al Thompson said. His voice was relieved and sad, both at once. "I knew you'd be down here somewhere."

The dock rocked as he stepped onto it. His face looked a lot older than yesterday, Dani thought. He came down to where Gwen was lying. Then he crouched and touched her cheek lightly. "Gwennie, love, wake up."

Gwen twitched, then groaned. She opened her eyes. Dani looked into them, but could see nothing of Sara there. It made her shiver how quickly Sara could disappear and leave her alone. "What time is it?" Gwen muttered.

Her father tried to smile. "Six. Did you sleep here all night?"

"I heard the loons," she said vaguely.

The birds called again, one of them or two, Dani wasn't sure which. Gwen started, turning swiftly onto her stomach to stare out at the water.

"They're not that far out. We could take the canoe out to see them," Mr. Thompson offered uncertainly.

"I always go by myself," Gwen said, without looking at him.

"You never used to. When you were little, I took you every morning—"

"That was then."

"Yes." Sadly. "I had more time then."

"No, you didn't." Still Gwen's eyes were fixed on the water, refusing to look at him. "We had lots of guests at the lodge in those days. You had less time, not more."

Mr. Thompson sat heavily down at the edge of the dock, so near to where Dani was perched that she scrambled to get out of the way. What would have happened if he *had* sat on her? Probably nothing. It was a discouraging thought.

Picking at a thread in his sleeve, Gwen's dad said, "Yes, you're right, Gwen. I had less time in those days. But we still went out in the canoe together to see the loons."

At last Gwen looked at him. "Don't you love them anymore, Dad?"

He turned a face so full of pain to her that Dani flinched. But Gwen's lips tightened, and she frowned. For the briefest of moments Dani could see Mrs. G in her. The look faded, and she was just another twelve-year-old

123

kid, pinched and unhappy, trying to understand. "If you do love them—" she began.

"I can't help it, Gwen," he got out, low and thick. "Sometimes you're pushed and you're pushed and you get to the point where you can't fight anymore, it's all too much for you, rotting docks and the business moldering away and the twins needing new shoes and the taxes to be paid and you mooning over a crystal that's as far out of reach as those loons out there . . ."

"*I* would fight," Gwen said. "I'd keep on fighting and fighting until there was nothing of me left."

"You would," her father said heavily. "I can't. Not anymore. I'm sorry."

For a long moment there was silence between them. The loons called again, a wilderness voice, lonely. Gwen looked very steadily at her knees. "I'm sorry I broke your birthday present, Dad."

He cleared his throat. "Some things can be fixed. There's a really good jeweler in Owen Sound. . . ."

Gwen began, very quietly, to cry.

✧

Sara didn't like crying, and never did very much of it, if she could help it. She had never imagined her grandmother crying at all. But here she was, doing it, and here Sara was, doing it with her. It wouldn't have been so bad if the crying had just been tears; she could have put up with that, like getting some grit in your eye and the tears coming automatically to wash it out. But this wasn't like that. Her grandmother's emotions were too strong; they invaded Sara's brain and heart, so that there was nothing Sara could do but feel.

Gwen pitied her father, and despised him, and yet somehow she still loved him. That was hard. Gwen hadn't known till now that such a thing was possible, and neither had Sara. People could be weak and do wrong things and still you could love them. And when they knew they were weak, and knew they'd done wrong things, and despised themselves for it as much as you did, maybe you had to love them even a little bit more.

It was why Gwen had said she was sorry for breaking her chain. Her father had lost too much. He had to be given something back. And so she gave it, and so she cried. And Sara cried with her, understanding for the first time something of what had made her grandmother the way she was.

I'll never be like him, Gwen vowed, deep within herself. I'll never let other people defeat me.

And you never have, Sara thought, suddenly proud. No, Grandma, you never have.

Gwen stopped crying. Her father was sitting quietly, not trying to comfort her, waiting. "Did you—say something?" she got out, with difficulty.

"Owen Sound," he said. "Do you want to come, or should I take the chain in by myself?"

"I broke it," Gwen said.

"We broke it together."

"Anyway, I should go."

"We could visit Uncle Ronnie on the way," her father said. He gave her a tiny, tentative smile. "And Thunder. If you like."

Gwen looked gravely at him. "All right."

He took a deep breath. Sara watched him. All at once she thought of Adam Duguay, stuck inside Gwen's father the way she was stuck inside Gwen. Had Duguay felt what Al Thompson must have felt, sitting there watching Gwen cry? Duguay was a Greysuit who knew icebreakers and oil wells, a man whose whole life was power and money. Until today, maybe, he had known nothing of what it was to be a man who loved loons, a man defeated by money and big business.

Like her, Sara thought. Like going outside and hating it but somehow still seeing it as beautiful, like crying because someone you love has done something bad — and because someone else you didn't even know you loved had done something brave and honorable and wise.

"Let's go now," Al Thompson said. "We can eat breakfast on the way."

✧

They were going to Uncle Ronnie's, Dani thought. They were going to see Thunder.

She clamped her hand around Gwen's wrist.

A horse. A real horse!

Hurry up, Dani thought. Let's go!

✧

It was a long way. The car was old and smelled of something chemical and made an awful noise, and Sara didn't like it one bit. It was better than being outside, but only marginally. She remembered sitting in the puffhover with the viewscreen open and the world spread out below her. This was less frightening than that, because the windshield of the car was dirty and mostly she could see only bits of the road ahead. On the other hand, in the puffhover she had been able to close her eyes. Sara tried now, but Gwen wanted to see. And so Sara watched with her.

She had never imagined that there could be this many dirt roads, trees, farms, and dusty little villages in the world. After an hour they ate breakfast in a place Mr. Thompson called a "greasy spoon," though it didn't look anything like a spoon to Sara. The food was unrecognizable, but it tasted fine. It was inside a building, and that was even better.

After breakfast Mr. Thompson did something smelly to the car. He used a hose, then paid another man with some bits of paper money. It was all very interesting in a scientific sort of way. Sara was almost not pleased when Gwen fell asleep again and she could no longer see anything. It wasn't very pleasant, sitting wide awake in Gwen's sleeping body and feeling the car move and hearing its noise and knowing that it was taking her farther and farther into the outside world. She wasn't even able to talk to Dani, with Mr. Thompson sitting right there.

Briefly, at the beginning of the long trip, she had wondered if Dani was with them at all. But then she remembered how Dani had told her about that picture she'd seen of Thunder, and how excited she'd been about it. No way was Dani going to miss out on seeing that horse in the flesh.

Sara wished she could sleep. But she didn't seem to need to. Images jumped around in her mind. Paper money, Grandma at the controls of the puffhover, loons, some eelgrass in an Arctic bay. Dani had been leading her by the arm there. Sara had never needed to be led around before. It had made her feel good at the time, but now she couldn't understand why.

Dani was so *certain* about things since they'd got here. It was all very well for her, with her "don't do anything, don't say anything, don't make Gwen do something she wouldn't do on her own." *Dani* could get up and move around. She could even walk through walls! Meanwhile Sara had to sit passively and wait for Gwen to think up something to do or something to say.

Boring, boring, boring! she told herself savagely, after at least an hour had passed.

127

I wonder, she thought suddenly, I wonder if I can make Gwen scratch her chin in her sleep.

She thought about fingers. She thought about arm muscles. She thought very, very hard about the distance between a hand and a chin. Slowly, very slowly, she felt Gwen's hand rise. Up, up—that's right—touch it—there! Now, scratch!

It worked! Sara thought gleefully. With slightly less effort, she made the fingers stop scratching, and the hand return to Gwen's lap.

Crossing her legs should be easy, after that, Sara thought. It wasn't, but she managed it.

"You waking up, Gwennie?" Mr. Thompson asked from the driver's seat.

"No-o-o," Sara said in Gwen's voice, and giggled to herself.

"We're almost to Ron's."

Wickedly, Sara made Gwen give a noise almost like a snore.

This is fun, she thought. She wondered if Dani guessed what she was doing. She wouldn't approve, of course. Well, too bad, Dani.

I *was* mean to her before, though, Sara thought contritely.

After that she remained quiet inside the sleeping Gwen's body, being good, and hoping Dani would know why.

The car's wheels changed sound. Dirt road again, Sara thought. They weren't on it long. The car stopped, the monstrous noise died away, and there was a faint crank-ing sound of the window being opened. Fresh air filled the car. "Good to see you, Ron," Gwen's father said.

"You too, Al. And hey, is that you over there, Gwennie?"

"She's out like a light. Poor kid's not been getting her eight hours lately. But I'll wake her if you think Tina—"

"Tina can wait to see her favorite niece. Meanwhile, you come on in. Looks like you could use a cold one."

"I suppose it won't hurt to let her sleep. Car's in the shade." The car door opened, and there was the sound of Mr. Thompson getting out. Then there came a click. He was trying to close the car door without waking Gwen, Sara thought. She wanted to yell, she was so happy he was going, but she supposed she had better restrain herself. She waited until the men's voices died away.

"Dani?" she whispered. "They gone yet?"

"Umm," Dani said.

"Dani?"

"Oh," Dani said. *"Oh."*

Sara could hear her gulping. "What is it? What's wrong? Are you sick? For heaven's sake, tell me!"

"It's—oh, Sara!—it's—" She gave a half sob. "That horse! Thunder! He's over in the meadow. He's—oh! Oh!"

Sara wanted to take her friend's hand. She wanted to hug her. Lucky Dani, who had never thought she would ever see a horse, lucky, lucky Dani to get this close to a living one. "Is he near?" she asked.

"And that mane, oh, it ripples when he—"

"Yes, but is he near?"

"He's nodding his head. Look, oh, look."

"I can't look, you idiot." Sara laughed. "My eyes are stuck."

"Would you mind if—? I mean, oh, Sara, I know you don't like to be alone outside, but you are in the car— it's not like it's really—"

"Go on, get out of here. Get as close to him as you can."

"Sugar!" Dani muttered wildly. "I need some sugar. He won't come to me without—"

"He won't come to you at all," Sara said. "You're invisible, remember? But *you* can go to *him*. Go on, Dani. Go!"

She waited for an answer, but there was none. "Dani?" No answer. Good. Dani was gone. Just for a moment, Sara felt lonely. But no. That wasn't fair. Dani had a right to this horse, after waiting for him all her life.

A long time passed. Sara counted Gwen's breaths. In. Out. In. Out. What was happening? For the first time Sara wished actively that she could see out. But she wouldn't be able to, not until Gwen woke up.

Or until somebody woke Gwen up.

It wouldn't change history to wake her up. Gwen woke up every day of her life, after all.

I'm going to do it, Sara decided. And then I'm going to make her look at Dani's horse.

Wake up! Sara screamed in Gwen's brain. *Wake up, Gwen! Wake up!*

Gwen yawned, stretched, opened her eyes. I'm in the car, she thought. We're at Uncle Ronnie's. She opened the car door.

No, Sara thought desperately. *Don't get out. Just look at the horse.*

But Gwen was already on her feet. Outside. The familiar dread filled Sara's mind, but this time she faced it. Okay, so she didn't like being outside. Okay. She'd survived it before, she'd survive it again. At least, if she was going to have to put up with it, she'd have a chance to see Dani's horse. But no. Gwen was looking toward a farmhouse, a big white building with bright red shingles on the roof. There was no meadow in her line of sight,

130

no plank fence, no horse. Gwen was thinking about her aunt Tina.

Turn your head, Sara willed her. *Turn it!* Nothing happened. Thunder, she urged. How's Thunder?

"Good old Thunder," Gwen murmured. She turned her head.

Sara turned hers, also. Yes. There. White plank fence, green pasture, a horse flying across the paddock, hooves kicking upward, ears flat. He was magnificent. Sara could see why Dani adored him. Okay, she had seen. Dani was right, he was beautiful. Okay. That's enough. Let's go.

"I wonder what's spooked him?" Gwen said. She frowned, then began to hurry toward the paddock.

Toward the house, not the horse! Sara said. Uncle Ronnie, she suggested guilefully to Gwen's brain. Aunt Tina.

Slowly, unwillingly, Gwen turned away from the paddock. But then Thunder began kicking the wooden fence every time he made a turn. It made a terrible racket. Gwen stared over her shoulder at him. Froth foamed from the stallion's mouth. He neighed, high and wild. "He'll hurt himself," Gwen said, suddenly frightened. "Thunder! Thunder, boy! Don't hurt yourself!"

She ran the rest of the way to the fence and began to climb it.

No! Sara screamed. *The house! Go to the house!* She screamed and screamed.

Gwen was shuddering now. Her hand slipped, then grabbed for another board. She had one leg over the fence; she scrambled for someplace to put her other foot.

Go back! Sara shouted at her.

Thunder turned, saw her. He was three-quarters of the way across the paddock, but Sara could see how his eyes were ringed with white. Gwen, too, saw those eyes. She froze.

The horse charged.

Sara shrieked. Gwen did not. She was paralyzed, five hundred kilograms of frenzied animal bearing down on her at the speed of a monorail, and still she was motionless, like someone in a trance.

Move! Sara willed her. *Fall backward! Get away!*

It was no good. Gwen did not hear.

She'll die, Sara thought despairingly. My grandmother's going to die, and it's all my fault. She won't live to get married and have my father. I'll never be born. History will be changed. I woke her up. I made her look at the horse. It's all my fault.

And then something happened. At the last minute, not three strides from the fence, the horse reared. It neighed violently, still rearing. Then, equally violently, it sheered off, clattering away to the far corner of the paddock, where it stopped, seeming almost to huddle into the fence, trying to get away. Steam rose from its body. Gwen dragged her leg back over the planks, fell to the ground, and was promptly and thoroughly sick.

✧

Dani couldn't cry. It wouldn't have mattered. No one could see her or hear her. But she couldn't cry.

My fault, she told herself, dry and sick. That dog was like that, too, when he sensed me. Oh. Oh, Thunder. I shouldn't have gone up to you. I shouldn't have tried to pat you. That's what spooked you. I should have known it would happen. I should have known.

Gwen was gone, stumbling over to the farmhouse, pounding on the door and being let in by her concerned family. She'd almost been killed. Would have been killed, Dani was sure, if she herself hadn't jumped in front of the horse. She was a ghost, she couldn't be hurt, but she

132

hadn't thought about that then, she'd only known she had to prevent these events she'd set in motion from carrying through to their terrible end. And it had worked. Thunder had veered away, and now he was pressed into the far fence, quaking and frothing with terror, doing anything rather than come any nearer to Dani, the ghost.

Dani dragged herself to the car. She didn't bother even trying the door, just pushed herself through it and lay down on the backseat. She didn't sleep. For a long time, she didn't move. And not once, not even when Gwen and her father got into the car and drove away, did Dani raise her head, not until they were far away from Uncle Ronnie's farmhouse, and the silver-grey horse called Thunder.

Chapter Twelve

THE jeweler's shop in Owen Sound was some distance off the busy main street. It was like no store Sara had ever seen. There was only one tiny showcase, and everything in it was made of gold: bracelets, chains, pins, and earrings, all in rather intricate designs. The rest of the shop looked like something Joshua might have dreamed up. A long bench held a cylindrical thing spouting blue flame, and there were glass tubes and sinks and presses and valves, hammers and tiny vises. Everywhere there were scraps of paper covered with drawings.

"He's an artist, not just a person who sells jewelry," Mr. Thompson explained in a whisper to Gwen. "He makes everything himself, and sells most of it in the big Toronto art galleries."

"You say you want this chain mended?" the man asked. He was old and wore a visor. He was squinting at the chain through a magnifying lens screwed into one eye. After a minute he peered up at Gwen. "Better off buying a new one, with a chain this fine. They're not very expensive."

"I don't want a new one," Gwen said. "I want this one."

Sara had known she was going to say that. The chain had to be fixed, because history required it to be.

"I'll do my best, but you'll see the mend," the man warned.

"I'm sure you'll do a fine job," Mr. Thompson said.

"All right, then," the jeweler said. "Won't take long, if you want to wait."

Gwen sat down quietly in the small visitor's area. She had been very subdued since the incident that morning with Thunder. After hearing her story, Uncle Ronnie had gone out to check on the horse and found him peacefully grazing. "Only thing I can think of is he got bit by some bug," Gwen's uncle told them, shaking his head. "Can drive a horse crazy, if he gets it in a sensitive spot. At least he didn't actually hurt you, Gwennie. He showed that much good sense."

He had suggested that they stay on for a few hours, just to be sure Gwen was all right, but she demurred. "I want to get my chain fixed," she kept saying, and finally her father had agreed. But now that they were at the shop she sat very straight and still and didn't show much interest in what the old man was doing. That didn't surprise Sara, who knew that Gwen's head was still full of questions about the morning's incidents.

She had been going straight to the house. Then, suddenly, she had decided to have a look at Thunder instead. Fair enough. She loved Thunder; always had. It was reasonable to look at him. But then what had happened to her? Deciding to do one thing and then suddenly doing another, turning toward the paddock, away from it, and then climbing that fence, and all that screaming?

It wasn't me, screaming, Gwen thought. It was somebody else. But there was no one else there. So it must have been me.

Sara shivered, knowing whose screaming it had been.

"But I never scream," Gwen muttered aloud.

"Pardon?" Al Thompson said.

Gwen shivered a little, sitting quietly in the visitor's chair in the jeweler's shop. "Nothing," she said.

Sara made herself as small and separate inside Gwen as she could. No more telling Gwen what to think and what to do. She'd got everyone into enough trouble by acting as if she owned Gwen's brain. "Don't make them do things," Dani had said. She'd been right about that. And I was so mean to her about it, Sara told herself guiltily.

Mr. Thompson seemed jumpy. He kept getting to his feet, wandering over to the jeweler's bench, picking up bits of equipment, putting them down again. Now and then the jeweler looked up from his work with pointed disapproval. Gwen began to pay attention. After a while she asked, "What's the matter, Dad?"

"Can't sit still, somehow," he said, frowning nervously. "Am I bothering you? Sorry."

"Why don't you read a magazine?"

He nodded vaguely, then plowed through the stack on a nearby table as if he knew exactly what he was looking for, stopping only when he got to a *National Geographic* with a cover picture of a seal sunning itself on an ice floe. This he pored over, not sitting down, seeming vitally interested in the information contained inside.

Arctic stuff, Sara thought. The North Pole. Was it Gwen's father who'd chosen to read the article, or was Adam Duguay forcing him to? She was afraid she knew the answer.

"I'd like to see the far north someday, Gwen," Mr. Thompson said intensely. "How about you?"

Gwen nodded. "Someday."

Sara wished she could tell the Greysuit how near to disaster they had all come this morning because she had forced Gwen to do things she didn't mean to do. Maybe he wouldn't be so free with his own forcing if he knew. Sara still shuddered to think what would have happened if that horse had not swerved away from Gwen at the last moment.

Why had he? It had seemed almost supernatural, the stallion pounding toward them on a killing course and then, barely a leap away, rearing up in the air and turning aside. What could have caused him to do that?

Dani would probably say that it was because of time not allowing the course of history to be changed. Sara tried to imagine some creature named Time jumping into that paddock swinging a big invisible whip and making Thunder veer off. It was pretty far-fetched, but Sara had made up her mind that she would no longer dismiss Dani's ideas without consideration.

Dani could see and do things in this century that neither Sara nor Duguay could do. That alone made her worth listening to. And there was something else. In this century Dani was supernatural, a bodiless being who didn't have to follow the normal laws. Maybe it made her more in tune with other things that weren't purely physical, things such as time.

"Here you are," the old jeweler said, holding out the chain. Gwen took it. The mend was clever, but nevertheless plainly visible. "Those links are tiny," the jeweler said. "I'm afraid a couple of them are fused together now."

"That's all right," Gwen said.

Her father reached into his breast pocket and took out the loon crystal. "Yours, I believe," he said. Somehow it was a question.

"Yes," Gwen said determinedly. She threaded it on the chain, then fastened it around her neck. A mirror hung nearby. She stood before it, and the pendant, reflected brilliantly in it, took fire, flashing a rainbow of colors into the dull workshop.

"Lovely work," the jeweler said approvingly, looking at the crystal.

Sara was scanning Gwen's face in the mirror. So that's what Grandma looked like when she was young, she thought. Pretty, in a bony kind of way, though her chin looked stubborn and her arms were muscular. Same blue eyes, of course, same dimple. Her hair was blond. Sara had never imagined it being anything but white.

Suddenly she wanted her grandmother back, she wanted her there, sharp-tongued and old-fashioned and the right grandmotherly age, telling Sara in no uncertain terms what and what not to do.

I wouldn't even argue with her, Sara told herself.

We've got to get *home*. The words repeated over and over in her brain. We've got to.

"You ready, Dad?" Gwen said, turning away from the mirror. "We've really got to be getting home."

❖

It was late afternoon when the old blue car pulled into the gravel parking area behind the lodge. Gwen's brothers, who were throwing sticks for Shags to fetch, came running to meet them. "Daddy, Daddy!" they called. "You get us anything in Owen Sound?"

"Well, *I* didn't," he said, getting out of the car, smiling. "However, your aunt and uncle sent you . . ." They piled on him happily. "Oof. Ow. Hope those chocolate-chip cookies didn't just get crushed. And unless I'm very much mistaken, this bag contains a couple of old Matchbox cars your cousin outgrew. . . ."

He opened the bag he was carrying and passed out the goodies. "And look, a hambone for Shags."

"Good old Aunt Tina," one of the boys said. "Hey, Shags, you got a bone."

Shags, who had barked joyously upon seeing the car pull in, now held back.

"Come on, Shags," Gwen called. "Bone, boy. Bone!"

139

The dog panted, his tongue hanging out, but instead of coming nearer, he slunk away into the undergrowth. "Better things to do, I guess," Mr. Thompson said with a shrug.

"That you, Al, Gwennie?" called Mrs. Thompson from inside the lodge. "I've got some hot cherry pie here, if you're hungry."

Gwen's dad grinned. "On our way!" He dropped the bag containing the bone on one of the chairs near the top step, and everyone disappeared into the house.

Dani climbed the stairs to the veranda. But she didn't want to go inside. Everyone in there belonged. She didn't.

After a while the door opened. "If anybody wants me, I'll be out here doing the accounts," Al Thompson said over his shoulder.

He was clutching a bag full of papers and a big blue book in one hand and a mug full of writing implements in the other. Drawing a chair up to a nearby table, he opened the blue book. Then he took a paper out of the bag, looked at it, frowned, wrote something in the book, and put the paper under the mug. Then he got out another paper from the bag and did the same thing all over again.

Dani watched him for some time, but the process was repetitive. Everything was repetitive when all you could do was watch. She began kicking one of her feet with the other. She wanted desperately to have somewhere to go, or something to do. If she could take out one of those canoes, for instance—but she knew she couldn't. If she couldn't even turn a doorknob, how could she paddle a canoe? How could she do anything useful, in this time and this place? How could she imagine herself as ever having been useful anywhere at all?

140

In a black mood she looked at the lake, watching the shadows lengthen.

A slight noise from behind made her turn. Al Thompson's head had dropped to his arms on the big blue book. He was snoring gently.

Dani went over to him. "Mr. Duguay?"

"Is that you, Dani? Or is it Sara?"

"Dani." She felt better now that there was someone to talk to.

"I'm beginning to understand a lot more things, Dani. Listen. I've been having a look at the accounts, and we're going to be getting quite a lot of money at the end of the month."

"We?" Dani asked dubiously.

"August 31, 1993," Duguay said. "It's when the first payment comes through on the lodge sale. With that kind of money we could charter a bush plane—I'm pretty sure they had bush planes in 1993—and go a long way north. From there, we could outfit an expedition to the Arctic. That magazine I read in Owen Sound mentioned a recent Arctic expedition—"

"Shh," Dani said quickly. "Someone's coming."

Gwen's mother opened the screen door. She saw Al, sound asleep, and smiled a little. Then, sighing, she came out and sat on the porch steps.

"She's going to stay," Dani said.

Duguay didn't even grunt. Dani waited. Minutes passed, but Dorrie Thompson didn't move. She seemed so peaceful, staring out at the lake. Dani thought of her own mother, and wished it were her, sitting there.

"I'm going to go look for Sara," she said aloud, knowing that only Duguay would hear.

She made her usual way into the lodge, and went

141

down to Gwen's room. Gwen was there, but she was reading to the twins. Dani listened. It was a story about a boy who lived in Ottawa and had to cross a place named Angel Square to get to school every day. There were all kinds of bullies there—Dani didn't understand their names—and something called the Shadow. The twins were enthralled by the book, but it baffled Dani, almost pained her. This was a story set in Ottawa, but it wasn't *her* Ottawa. There was nothing about it that she could recognize at all. She left Gwen's room and went back out onto the veranda.

Mrs. Thompson was gone. But Al was still there. And he was still asleep. But now, instead of being asleep sitting at the table with his head on his arms, he was walking.

Dani knew he was asleep because she could hear Adam Duguay talking. "Step. That's it, Al. Left. Right. That's it. Go."

"Mr. Duguay!" she said, outraged. "What are you doing?"

Duguay's attention must have faltered. Either that or he tried to move Al Thompson's body too abruptly. Whatever happened, Al woke up.

For a moment he stood there, half in a stupor. Then he yawned. "Woozy," he muttered. He took a few deep breaths, rubbed his eyes hard, then looked at his watch. "Getting late," he said. "Now, did I—?"

He went over to the table, ran his finger down a column of figures in the blue book, shook his head. "Time to call it a day." He gathered everything up, including the paper bag that had the hambone in it. "Whew," he said, wrinkling his nose at the smell. "Shags! Hey, Shags! Come get your bone before I throw it out."

The dog did not appear. Al shrugged, unwrapped the

142

bone, made a face at it, then dropped it on the top step, and took the rest of the things into the house.

Dani supposed she should follow him. There wasn't anything else to do, after all. Slowly she crossed the veranda, but then she rebelled. She went back to the stairs, sank to the top step, and sat there, her chin in her hand, just as Dorrie Thompson had sat earlier. The hambone lay beside her, smelling very strong.

The horse, Thunder, had smelled, too. To Dani his had been a brand-new smell, like a combination of dry grass and the edginess of Arctic seaweed with a whiff of rollerclothes after a week in the gym bag. His breath had been hot and not at all sweet, especially when the foam started coming and his steaming body made strings in his silver mane.

But he had been beautiful. Before she had touched him, before he had become aware of her and gotten so afraid, he had been beautiful.

A low whine at the foot of the steps made her lift her chin from her hands. There was the dog Shags, staring longingly up at the hambone.

"You'd better run away," she said aloud to him, drearily. "I'm here, too. The big bad ghost. Boo." She put her chin back in her hand.

She had imagined it all as being so different. She had imagined herself and the horse coming together like old friends. Instead she'd scared the poor animal to a frenzy.

Another whine. Shags, again. His ears were cocked anxiously. He must really want his bone, she thought. "I never knew any dogs," she said to him, very formally. "I'm sorry if I did things wrong when I met you the first time. If you're that hungry, I'll go away, and then you can have your bone." She got up, very slowly. The dog tensed. "It's all right, I'm not coming near you," she said. "Look, I'm going way over to that chair over there." His body relaxed a little as she made her way to the chair, backward, watching him as she went.

When she was sitting, Shags suddenly darted up the steps, closed his jaws around the bone, and ran back down again. Dani watched him disappear into the bushes.

The only two creatures in this century who knew she was here hated her.

Dry-eyed, she sat in the chair. She sat there for a long, long time. The sun set behind the hill; twilight drew on. Someone lit the lights in the lodge. Someone else drew the curtains. Slowly her stomach stopped feeling so sick. Inside the lodge people were laughing; the twins were having a good-natured shouting match. To Dani it all seemed far away. Here on the quiet veranda she felt as isolated as if she were encased in crystal. Night was falling; the moon was rising. She imagined a perfect loon floating motionless in a perfect lake. She closed her eyes. Silence descended. Peace.

A sawmill in this place. Just thinking of its coming conjured it up for Dani, huge and ugly, rocks barren around it, the trees and the moss all gone. Saws screaming, stench, the trampling of the undergrowth, gaping cement pipes vomiting horrible things into the water.

Poor loons.

Poor Gwen.

Poor Mr. Thompson, who would never dare return to see what he had done.

I can see it, Dani thought. I know what it's going to be like.

Crystal clear in her mind's eye, she saw heat rising off a blockbuilding roof, an Ottawa river bubbling with

144

chemicals, Parliament Hill with its painted green pavement empty of trees, Verdant Meadows with its greenery enclosed in a plastic prison. This was what was waiting for her when she went home. This was what was waiting for everyone.

It was the animals Dani was sorriest for. They hadn't made it happen, but they were going to suffer the consequences anyway. Those loons. Poor, beautiful Thunder, whose kind would be reduced to a holograph on a bedroom wall. Even dogs like Shags, who would probably be in a pet zoo if he lived in Dani's world.

Some rich people in Dani's century had pets of their own, but ordinary people never did. Pets were expensive, and laws had been passed against their droppings. Dani thought of the twins laughing and throwing sticks to Shags; of Shags keeping guard in their room; of how he waited faithfully on Gwen's bed until she came to cuddle him. Shags loved his humans, plainly. What a terrible loss to the ordinary people of Dani's world never to know the love of a creature like Shags.

She heard a sound. She opened her eyes. Shags was there, right there at her feet, looking up at her.

She didn't say a thing. She didn't dare. Slowly, the dog sat back on his haunches. For a long, long time, he watched her carefully. She watched him right back, not moving. Then, at last, the dog seemed to make up his mind. He sighed, then lay down at her feet, his nose on his paws. Now and then he lifted his head again, his eyes seeking her out. But still he didn't move away.

For endless minutes Dani sat very still. She didn't make a sound, though something sang inside her. The lake glimmered in the moonlight. Blue shadows trembled under the trees near the lodge. The next time the dog lifted his head to look at her, the white rim around his eyes had disappeared. When he dropped his head to his paws again, this time he slept.

Good dog, Shags. Oh, good, good dog.

Inside the lodge, someone was playing music. People were singing. "Time for bed, boys," Mrs. Thompson commanded, uselessly. Out on the lake, a loon called to its mate. Crystal water broke into a circle of ripples.

Gwen can't hear the loons, Dani thought. None of them can. They're inside in their own little world, and the loons are out here, all of this is out here, and they don't even know.

I wish I could stay here forever, Dani thought, suddenly and fiercely. Shags here, knowing me and not minding; this perfect place—oh, I wish this moment could last forever!

But even as she wished it, things changed. A cloud covered the moon. The night grew cool and darker. The lake turned from silver to black. The loons disappeared from hearing.

It didn't matter what you wanted, sooner or later, things would change.

Time was like that. It had its own rules. And one of those rules was for Dani and Sara and Adam Duguay to be in their own century and their own place when the time came on the deck of an icebreaker to decide the future of the Arctic.

You couldn't change history, Dani thought.

You couldn't change what had already happened.

The only thing you could do, if you worked really hard, and tried really hard, was to change the future.

Chapter Thirteen

I T was hours later when Shags woke, lifting his head into the moonlight, then casually rising and padding off. Dani didn't mind. His lying by her feet had accomplished what nothing else had been able to do, all the time she had been in this strange century. For days, it seemed, she had run here and run there, up the hill to Gwen's secret place, down to the dock, through walls and into people's bedrooms and cars and paddocks and jewelry stores. For days, it seemed, she had explored and listened and observed and talked, objecting to Sara's ideas, worrying about Duguay's, being certain inside herself of what was wrong about them without being at all certain what was right. What she hadn't done was sit very calmly and just think.

And then a big, rumpled old dog had paid her the compliment of lying by her feet, and rather than disturb him, she had simply sat. She hadn't gone to Sara, who would be lying in Gwen's sleeping body wondering where she was and wanting more talk, more arguments. She hadn't gone to Adam Duguay, who would be full of ways to force Al Thompson to take them to the North Pole. She had just sat there, allowing herself to think, to imagine that she alone, by herself, could come up with some answers. And slowly, over the hours, the answers had come.

Time had its own rules. That had always been the clue. Time would not allow the past to be changed. That was why she was a time ghost. It was why Sara was inside

147

Gwen, and Adam Duguay was inside Gwen's dad. In these forms time tried to ensure that the three of them from the future could not do anything that would change the past.

But they could do some things. Dani could speak to Shags and know that he heard, and she could get a reaction from Thunder. Duguay could make Gwen's dad walk in his sleep, and he could make him look at a magazine and say he'd like to see the far north. Dani was pretty sure Sara had made Gwen give that snoring noise in the car this morning. None of those things were major enough to change history. But scaring a horse into attacking Gwen: that was major. That could have changed history. And so it had had to be stopped. And it had been.

Time would not allow the past to be changed. Dani had known it, but not until now had she understood the full implications of that principle. Time would not *allow* the past to be changed.

Gwen had never been in danger of dying this morning. Dani had thrown herself in front of Thunder, and maybe that had made the stallion veer, but if she hadn't, something else would have. Gwen couldn't be allowed to die. Time would not allow it.

Gwen's chain was mended now. That was as it should be. Broken once in this century, mended once. Sara had said they should break it again at the North Pole, and that would get them home. Dani had worried about that, without understanding why. She had thought it was just that it was wrong to try to make Mr. Thompson and Gwen go to the North Pole, when in their proper lives they would do no such thing. Yes, that had been wrong, but it was not the only thing. The real thing wrong with what Sara had suggested was that they couldn't be allowed to break the chain again at all.

148

That chain had been broken only once in this century, not twice. If Sara and Duguay tried to make Gwen and her father break that chain again, they would fail. They would have to fail. Time would not allow that chain to be broken twice. Whether Sara and Duguay tried to do it at the North Pole or here, time would stop them.

And the easiest, the most logical way to stop them would be to remove them from this century altogether. Send them back where they belonged, where they had to be to complete the actions that had begun on the deck of the *Seabeater*.

It was so obvious, Dani marveled. So perfectly straightforward.

Try to break the chain. Try it here at the lake, on the dock, where it had happened the first time, everything the same as before so that if time *did* send them back, it would be to the deck of the *Seabeater*, not somewhere else. Repeat everything: Sara making Gwen pull at the chain while Duguay hooked Al's finger in it and made him pull the other way; and Dani, of course, carefully holding tight to Gwen's wrist with one hand while hooking her other in Al's free arm. Try to break the chain. Really try, and see.

The chain would *not* break, of that Dani was sure. Something would happen to stop it. And if it were the right thing, she and Sara and Duguay would all be back in their own time.

She got to her feet and went to find Sara.

❖

"But what if you're wrong?" Sara said. "What if we try to break the chain and it doesn't send us back to the future?"

"We won't be any worse off than we are now," Dani

replied. "That chain won't break again, I'm sure of it. Whatever happens, we won't change history by trying."

"But we will change history if Gwen and her father get into another argument," Sara said. "Face it, Dani. It would take the fight of the century to get Gwen and her father to break that chain again after it's only just been fixed."

"That's just why it can't be Gwen and Al who are really trying to break it," Dani said. "It has to be you and Duguay, not them at all."

Sara heaved an exasperated sigh. "How *can* it be just us breaking that chain, Dani? You know we only have Gwen's and Al's bodies to work with! If *we're* doing it, *they're* doing it."

"Well, yes, in a way. But they wouldn't need a reason like an argument to be trying to break it if they were doing it in their sleep, would they?"

Sara was so surprised that Gwen's mouth dropped open. "You mean," Sara whispered, half horrified, half fascinated, "we've got to get Gwen and Al down to that dock *in their sleep,* and then we've got to get them to try to break that chain, all without waking them up?"

"You *can* make them do things in their sleep," Dani pointed out. "At least, Mr. Duguay can make Al. He was making him sleepwalk just this afternoon. And I thought maybe that in the car you—"

"Yes," Sara said hastily.

"Doing it in their sleep is the only way I can think of to make sure that it'd be us time has to stop, not Gwen and her dad. The best way to stop *us* would be to send us back to our own time. Who knows what the best way to stop them would be?"

There was a long, respectful silence. Then Sara said, "You really have thought it all through, haven't you? Boy,

Dani, the next time you say you don't get good ideas, I'm going to remind you of this."

"We don't know for sure that it'll work," Dani cautioned.

"It's the best thing any of us has been able to come up with." She paused. "It'll be hard, though."

"I know. Gwen's not even wearing her pendant."

"If you're right, I'll have to get her to put it on in her sleep. I'll have to make her do *everything* in her sleep." Her voice sounded strange, Dani thought. Almost afraid. "Are we going to do it now?"

It was odd, Dani thought, to have Sara leaving the decisions to her. "I don't see any reason to wait," she said, "do you?"

"I guess not." Another long pause. "What'll happen," Sara wondered aloud, "when we go back to the future —if we do—and Gwen and Al are left standing asleep on the dock in the middle of the night?"

"Nothing major," Dani said confidently. "Time will take care of that. Maybe they'll just sleepwalk back to bed. Or maybe they'll wake up and think they've each come down to look at the stars or something. Remember, the chain *won't* be broken. They won't have to have an argument."

"Have you told Duguay your plan?"

"Not yet."

"It's the middle of the night. Al's sure to be asleep. Dorrie, too. As long as Duguay doesn't talk too much, you could get in there and tell him without her waking, probably. If you wanted to, that is."

Again Sara was leaving it up to her, not telling her what to do. "Okay," Dani said. "And you could be getting Gwen to put on that pendant while I do. If *you* wanted to, that is."

Sara gave a little laugh. That was all, but Dani felt really good, suddenly.

"I'm going now," she said to Sara. "I'll see you on the dock. Good luck with Gwen."

"I'll need it," Sara said, as if she really meant it. Again, Dani thought she sounded scared. But her mind was on Duguay now: telling him, getting him to agree.

Quietly, as Dani turned to go, Sara called, "Hey, Dani?"

"What?"

"Nothing. I mean—best friends forever, huh?"

"What else?" Dani said, smiling, and left.

✧

It was hard getting Gwen out of bed, a lot harder than just making her scratch her chin in her sleep, or cross her legs and give a snoring noise. But Duguay had succeeded in making Gwen's father sleepwalk, and what a Greysuit could do, Sara Melody Green wasn't going to fail at.

It was accomplished at last. Sound asleep, Gwen stood on her feet. Now for the hard part. Gwen had to open her eyes, or Sara would not be able to see where to guide her.

Sara knew that sleepwalkers often remained asleep even when their eyes were open, but she didn't understand how. She thought about it, hard. A lullaby, she thought. Quietly, she began to hum one into Gwen's mind. It was one her father had sung to her when she was little. *Bye, bye, baby, sleep like a lady. . . .*

That's right, Gwen. Sleep like a lady. Don't pay any attention to your eyes. Just sleep.

I will be with you, she sang, *when morning time is here.*

And all the time she sang it she thought about Gwen's eyelids, and the mechanism for opening them.

152

The eyelids fluttered. At the same time, something in Gwen's mind struggled for alertness.

No, Sara thought. No. She sang on. *Sleep like a lady. I will be with you when morning time is here.*

I hope I won't, Sara thought fiercely. Again that thing struggled in Gwen's mind. Sara controlled herself. Fierceness wasn't smart. Fierceness wouldn't make Gwen stay asleep. It was gentleness she needed, coziness, sleepy-time cuddles, love.

And anyway, Sara told herself, she *would* be with Gwen when morning was here, even if Dani's plan worked. She'd be with the Gwen who would have grown up into Grandma. Not the difficult old Grandma who was always causing trouble for someone, but the Grandma who had loved her home and seen it destroyed, the Grandma who had vowed to fight and fight until there was nothing of her left. Sara understood that Grandma.

Bye, bye, baby, she sang, softly now, lovingly. The thing in Gwen's mind drifted off again. *Sleep like a lady.* Gwen slept.

Open your eyes, Sara willed, gentle but stern. Open them. Now.

Gwen's eyelids opened, but that thing in her mind stayed asleep.

I can see, Sara thought. She's asleep, and I can see.

It was dark in the room, but not pitch-black. After a few minutes Sara could make out the dresser where Gwen had dropped the pendant when she'd gone to bed that night. She made Gwen's arm lift, her fingers reaching for the pendant.

Good thing I practiced on her in the car, Sara thought.

She didn't let herself think too far ahead. Doing up the pendant was hard. Even at home in the twenty-first century Sara had needed Grandma's help to get it on. But there was no one to help her now. She wanted to scream at the clumsiness of Gwen's sleeping fingers, but finally the little hook caught. She had done it. The pendant was on. She had done it by herself.

By herself. As she was going to have to take Gwen's sleeping body, by herself, down to the dock.

Outside.

It was the next thing. She had to do it. Eyes wide open, forced to see. Doing it herself, Sara forcing Gwen instead of the other way around.

Sara choosing on her own to go outside by herself.

I can't do it, Sara thought.

But she had to.

Gwen's eyes stared into the darkness. Sara stared through them. I have to go, Sara told herself. I have to go, and I have to look, or I'll never find the way.

"I would fight," Grandma had said, or Gwen, or both of them together. "I'd keep on fighting and fighting until there was nothing of me left."

In my world, I'm a fighter, too, Sara told herself. It's only when I have to go outside—

But Grandma was a fighter inside and out.

Sara took a deep breath. All right, then, Grandma, she said, all right, let's go.

And to keep her spirits up, as much as to keep Gwen asleep, she sang.

> *Bye, bye, baby, sleep like a lady,*
> *I will be with you when morning time is here.*

And it came to her then, as she maneuvered Gwen's body down the corridor, heading for the outside door, that Dad must have learned that lullaby from Grandma singing it to him when he was small and tired and needed comforting. And he had grown up and sung it to Sara for the same reasons, and she had learned it from him. And now here she was singing it to Grandma again.

Everybody comforting everybody else, Sara thought, everybody *connected*.

It was like being a link in an unbreakable chain. It made her feel strong.

✧

"Don't say anything," Dani told Adam Duguay, "not unless you make it very quiet."

The room was dim, but Dani could see. Dorrie Thompson lay on her stomach, her hair spilling over the pillow. She was breathing heavily, deeply asleep, as Sara had predicted. Al Thompson was on his back, his mouth open, eyes closed.

There was a low grunt from Duguay, just enough to reassure Dani that he was listening. "We both know you can make Al sleepwalk," Dani continued. "I want you to do it again. Down to the dock. As soon as you can."

She paused, waiting.

"Why?" Barely audible.

Dani's heart beat faster. "I think I know how to get us all back to our own time," she said. "But I'm not going to tell you, not unless you promise me something."

Again she waited. "I won't promise until I know what you want," Duguay muttered at last. "I'll find my own way back, if I have to." His voice was louder, but Dorrie never moved. Neither did Al.

"It's about this lake, Mr. Duguay," Dani said. "You've seen it. You know what it's like. Is it worth saving?"

"I can't save it. Even Al can't save it. It's too late. The contract's signed."

"But if you could—"

"Hypothetical situations are a waste of time."

155

"Mr. Duguay, do you *like* the lake?"

He was silent. Then, as if it cost him something important, he said, "It's—fine."

"It's going to die. We both know that. The trees are going to be cut down, and the loons will disappear. The lake won't be beautiful anymore. It'll be like—Ottawa."

"You said I had to promise something," he muttered after a moment.

She swallowed, hard. But she had thought about this a long time. She had to ask him. "Al Thompson isn't happy about what he's done, Mr. Duguay. And you're inside him. I know you like icebreakers and oil wells and things like that. You probably even like mills. But what I want to know is, are you happy about *this* mill and what it's going to do *here*?"

She waited. She waited for a long time. At last, almost resentfully, Adam Duguay replied. "No, I'm not happy about it. But is that me, or is it just Al making me feel that way?"

"It doesn't matter," Dani said. "You feel it. That's what I wanted to know."

"And the promise?"

"Just—remember. Remember this place, and remember the loons. Remember what's going to happen here, because of people only caring about money."

Another long pause. Then Duguay said, "All right. I'll remember. I promise."

Dani pictured the man on board the *Seabeater*, his direct grey gaze, his firm mouth. She believed him. "I'll tell you how I think we can get home," she said.

She explained it quickly. He listened. At the end of it, he murmured thoughtfully, "You know, it just might work."

"You and Sara would really have to mean to break the chain," she warned him. "Pretending wouldn't do it, or time wouldn't be forced to stop it from happening."

"I understand," he said.

"And you wouldn't be able to let Al wake up while you were doing it in case time stopped him instead of—"

"I said I understood." He added softly, "You're a bright little thing, aren't you? I wonder why you didn't just leave me here, and go yourselves, you and Sara? If you're right, all it would take is for Sara to try to break the chain, with you holding onto her. You didn't have to include me in this at all."

"How could we be sure to get back to the *Seabeater* unless we're all together, the way we were when we left? Anyway," she added in a low voice, "I know what it's like to be alone here."

"Thanks," he said.

She turned away. "I'll be going now, Mr. Duguay. Sara will be down on the dock soon."

"So will I," he said calmly, "just as soon as I can."

✧

It took longer than Dani had hoped. She waited on the dock, and waited, but neither Sara nor Duguay came. The eastern sky began to brighten, though it was still night everywhere else. Dani paced the dock, staring alternately out at the silvering lake and back at the dark bulk of the lodge. What was taking them so long? Had Gwen wakened while Sara tried to make her sleepwalk? Had Al? Where were they? Why didn't they come?

She had almost made up her mind to go back up to look for them when she heard footsteps on the stairs leading down to the dock. She strained her eyes into the gloom. "Sara?" she called. "Is that you?"

157

"Me," Duguay said.

She could see him now. Al Thompson's eyes were open, but his arms were in front of him and he was staggering a little, like someone who'd almost forgotten how to walk. Dani wanted to take his arm, but knew it wouldn't help. He wouldn't even feel it. Anxiously she watched as he maneuvered his way onto the dock, took a few steps forward, and stopped.

"Are you okay?" she asked.

"Tired," Duguay grunted. Dani guessed it had been very hard work, getting the other man to walk so far without waking him.

More time passed. The sky grew rosy. The lake brightened. A light breeze just barely ruffled the water. "Where *is* she?" Duguay muttered.

Dani said, "I think I'll—" She broke off. "Sara! Thank heavens!"

Gwen's body was jerking down the steps to the dock. All her grace was gone. Her eyes were wide and staring, her mind plainly asleep. *"I will be with you when morning time is here."*

Was Sara singing? Surely not!

But she was. *"Bye, bye, baby . . ."* An exhausted singsong voice going on and on. Dani scanned the open-necked nightgown Gwen was wearing, praying that she would see the pendant. There! Sara had managed it!

"You're here, Sara," Dani whispered. "You made it. You're on the dock."

Gwen stopped moving. Sara stopped singing. "Dani?"

"It took you so long," Dani said. "I was scared—"

"I was, too. Now I'm just tired."

"You're almost done," Dani encouraged her. "All we have to do—"

158

"Oh," Sara said. Gwen's body was standing perfectly still, her open eyes facing the lake.

"What?" Dani asked.

"The water. It's—"

"What?"

"I never saw water that color before. It's silver. The way it is in my pendant." Slowly, with great effort, Sara moved her hand to her chest, then closed it around the pendant. She tried to lift it to her eyes, but the chain was too short. "It is like my pendant, isn't it, Dani? Silver, with that tree over there just like the one in—"

"We should be doing what we came here to do," Adam Duguay said.

Dani was watching Gwen: asleep, but with Sara's awareness looking out of her eyes. There was something different about her. Sara was outside, and for the first time she wasn't afraid.

"It *is* like my pendant, isn't it?" Sara insisted. "Look at it, Dani. It is."

Dani looked from the pendant to the lake, and back to the pendant again. A tiny maple tree beside a silver lake, ripples on the water. "Just like it," she assured Sara. "There isn't any loon, but except for that—"

Duguay spoke again. "Dorrie will be getting up soon."

He was right. They should do it now. But if everything worked the way they hoped, this would be their last chance to see the lake. Once they were gone, they would never look on it again. The people whose bodies they left behind would have it for a while longer, but soon it would be gone for them, too. "Just one moment more, Mr. Duguay," Dani whispered.

He was silent. The three of them stood there watching dawn bring color to the distant shoreline. Trees, Dani thought hungrily, memorizing them. Endless clean water, here smooth as glass, there with those gentle little ripples. A fish leaping. Sunlight unrolling a glittering path across the lake, shore to shore, dazzling. Green, and blue, and pink, and white, Dani thought; silver turning to gold, the smell of pines, the warmth of sunlight on her skin.

"It's beautiful," Sara murmured slowly. "It really is beautiful."

Dani closed her eyes. The image was in her mind. It would always be in her mind. She took a deep breath, turned her back on the lake, and let herself see again. "Ready, everyone?"

"Ready," Duguay said. Al Thompson took two steps, three. Slowly Sara turned Gwen's body away from the lake to face him.

"Hook his finger under her chain," Dani said.

The man's hand went out. Slowly his index finger uncurled from his palm. "Sara?" Dani said. "Are you ready to pull?"

"Put your hand on my wrist, Dani."

Dani obeyed. As she closed her hand around Gwen's wrist, Dani could feel the enormous effort Sara was making as she struggled with Gwen's muscles, holding the pendant aloft. "You're going to break the chain. Remember that. You've got to really mean to."

She waited. Neither Sara nor Duguay said anything. "All right, then. One, two, three, *pull.*"

Chapter Fourteen

"*SARA!*" Mrs. G's voice sounded horrified. "What are you *doing?*"

In the deepening twilight of an Arctic afternoon, Dani looked at Sara's grandmother, whose face under her wind-whipped hair was rigid with shock and anger. Dani looked at Sara, to whose wrist she still clung. She looked at Adam Duguay, standing solid and still, his grey eyes narrow. She looked beyond them all, to Karl and Josh, heading curiously for them down the deck of the *Seabeater.*

White-faced, Sara stared, too, but at Adam Duguay, not her grandmother. Her hand held the pendant tightly, the broken chain dangling.

"We broke it," she said. She added faintly, "But we're back, anyway."

Duguay shook his head slightly. "We broke it here," he told her urgently, and so quietly that only Dani and Sara could make out the words. "This century. Not back on the dock."

Dani understood. Of course. Back in the twentieth century, Gwen still had her pendant hanging from her neck, the chain unbroken. The threat to break it had been enough. Time had brought them back to their own century. But in their own century they *had* broken Sara's pendant. It was why they had gone into the past in the first place. And now they had returned to the twenty-first century, after all that time in 1993, and apparently almost no time had passed here at all. Here the chain

161

that held Sara's pendant had just been broken, and the consequences were still to be faced.

Mrs. G left the rail and marched to Sara's side. Her lips were thin, and her voice very cold. "Your pendant. Oh, how could you, Sara?"

"I'm sorry—oh, Grandma—I'm so sorry!"

Dani dropped her hand from Sara's wrist, reaching out unthinkingly for Mrs. G. "She was afraid—she hated being outside—please, Mrs. G—"

But Mrs. G ignored Dani. Suddenly she was ignoring Sara, too. Her back was very erect. She faced Adam Duguay. "I'm so sorry, Mr. Duguay. My granddaughter has behaved very badly to you."

Adam Duguay said nothing for a moment. He only looked at Mrs. G, whose eyes blazed proudly even as she apologized. "She didn't want to show me her pendant," he said at last, as if reminding himself of something that had happened a long time ago. "No reason why she should have to. It was *her* pendant."

Mrs. G flushed. "You had never seen a loon," she said, defending herself from his unspoken accusation. "I thought you should see one, even if it was only the one in Sara's pendant. In any case, there is no excuse for rudeness. Sara will apologize, naturally."

"I'm very sorry I was rude," Sara said, very quickly. Her voice broke. "And, oh, Grandma, I'm sorry I broke my birthday present. Your lake, your beautiful lake . . . "

"We can discuss that another time," Mrs. G said. "I'm sure Mr. Duguay feels very uncomfortable in the middle of a family quarrel."

"I've been in family quarrels before," Duguay said.

Josh and Karl arrived, Karl first, frowning. "Sara's crying. What's going on?"

"I'm not crying," Sara said, her voice muffled.

"Your nose is all splotchy." Karl's voice was stiff. He looked at his grandmother, then at Duguay. "Sara doesn't ever cry."

"Those birds we heard, Mrs. G," Josh put in tactfully, "were they loons?"

Mrs. G strode over to the rail, turned with her back to it, and faced them like the judge she had been. "Sara broke the pendant I gave her," Mrs. G said coldly. "She did it deliberately. That's what's going on, Karl. And yes, Joshua, they were loons."

"I was angry," Sara said pleadingly to her grandmother. "When I first saw the pendant I thought you gave it to me to make me like the things you do. You know, the outside, nature, things like that. And then—"

"I don't give birthday presents to force people to do things. I gave you the pendant because you are my granddaughter and it's your birthday and I love you."

Her words seemed to echo. She blinked, an uncertain frown furrowing her forehead. Dani watched her, remembering Al Thompson on a dock, hurt and pleading: *I got it for you because you are my daughter and it's your birthday and I love you.* Was Mrs. G remembering that, too? Was she looking back all those years to when she was twelve years old and furious, a pendant she saw as a bribe dangling from her finger?

Sara lifted her chin. It was wobbling. "I was angry," she said again, her voice thick. "You kept forcing me to go outside. You knew I was scared, but you kept—"

"You said you were sick." Mrs. G the judge, Dani thought. She took Sara's arm and hugged it to her.

"But you knew she wasn't really sick, Grandma," Karl put in, still oddly stiff. "We all knew she was just scared. And you did force her. Sara's right about that."

"This is neither the time nor the place to—" Mrs. G began.

163

"You do order people around sometimes, Grandma," Karl went doggedly on, his color high. "You do it with me, too. Sara's just the same. It drives me crazy sometimes. You on one side, her on the other. No wonder you don't get along."

Dani stole a quick glance at Duguay, who was looking down at his folded hands, seeming not to be at all interested in what was going on. Mrs. G looked at him, too. But Karl labored on.

"The thing is—well, look, Sara doesn't cry. And now she's—"

"I am *not* crying," Sara said with desperate dignity. She followed her grandmother over to the rail and touched her sleeve. "Grandma, now I know why you gave me the pendant. I was missing something before—a lot of things, really—and you knew it. I'm sorry I had to break your birthday present to find that out for myself, but at least I did find it out. Grandma, I know it isn't an excuse, but sometimes you're pushed and you're pushed and you get to the point—"

Again Mrs. G. looked taken aback.

"Mrs. Green—"

It was Adam Duguay. Everyone turned to him. "I know it's none of my business, but I think you should forgive your granddaughter. Obviously she is sorry. I don't think she knew the consequences of her actions before she—"

"She ought to have," Mrs. G interrupted. "People have to understand that everything they do has consequences. They have to take responsibility."

Dani looked back and forth from one of their faces to the other. She knew that they weren't just talking about Sara's broken chain.

"Can't the chain be fixed?" Josh asked practically.

"Some things, once they're ruined, can never be fixed," Mrs. G said.

Sara looked miserably at the deck.

"Yes, of course, Mrs. Green, you're perfectly right," Duguay said. "But some things can be. It's important to distinguish, don't you think?"

"Well, I don't know," Mrs. G said.

It was the first time Dani had ever heard her say anything like that. Sara, too, must have taken hope from it, for clutching the pendant in her fist, she suddenly threw both arms around her grandmother. "Grandma, I'm sorry. Please, oh, it's the loveliest, most perfect gift, and I've broken it, I know, but just the chain, not the pendant, and a chain can be mended—"

"Oh dear," Mrs. G said helplessly. "I suppose . . ."

Karl cleared his throat. He looked at Sara, who was beginning to smile. His expression smoothed over. "But if she *did* break it on purpose . . ." he began.

Dani glared at him. First he stuck up for Sara, and then, when it finally seemed as if Mrs. G might be going to cave in, he had to go and start things up again. What was the matter with him?

She said, "Haven't *you* ever broken anything on purpose, Karl? Maybe because you were really angry?" She turned to Sara's grandmother. But she wasn't just Sara's grandmother, Dani reminded herself, she was Gwen, too. Dani took a deep breath. "You can understand how someone might do that, can't you, Mrs. G? Break something they loved on purpose, I mean, just because they were angry?"

Josh said, "Don't be stupid, Dani. Mrs. G wouldn't understand a dumb thing like that."

Mrs. G peered uncertainly at Dani. Then she sighed. "I'm sorry, Josh, but I would. I did it myself—to this very chain, actually—a long time ago." She shrugged a little at his expression, then smiled at Sara. "All right," she said. "Chains can be fixed. All right."

Sara closed her eyes briefly, then took a big breath. "Thanks, Grandma." Her voice was solemn. "I promise I'll never break your chain again."

"I'm sure you won't," her grandmother said. Then she, too, took a breath. "Mr. Duguay, I have to apologize again. I intended for us to be well into our business discussions by now, but instead we've all been wasting your time—"

"It hasn't been a waste of time," Duguay said, stepping forward. He was looking at Mrs. G as if he were trying to figure out some hard question in mental arithmetic. "Your name was Thompson, wasn't it, before you were married?"

So he'd figured it out, Dani thought. She had never told him that Mrs. G and Gwen were one and the same; somehow there just never had been the right time. But now he knew. What would he do? Surely he wouldn't tell Mrs. G that in 1993 he had been inside her father!

"That's right, my maiden name was Thompson," Mrs. G said, nodding coolly. "What of it?"

"Nothing, really," Duguay answered. "I was just thinking of someone you reminded me of. Someone I knew a long time ago."

"Mr. Duguay," Mrs. G said tartly, "we really ought to be sitting down to some serious discussions instead of wasting time on my character, or that of someone you once knew."

"Then you don't subscribe to the theory that it's better to know as much as you can of the person you have to deal with?"

"I hardly think it will affect our opposite positions on oil in the Arctic."

"No? Well, time will tell." Adam Duguay smiled thoughtfully. "Shall I send for a sailor to take us over to your puffhover now?"

"It'll mean these dreadful children taking over your decks," Mrs. G warned.

"I promised them they could do their experiments," Duguay said. He looked directly at Dani. "And I always keep my promises."

Dani knew what that meant. Her promise. The one she had made him make, back at the lake before she would tell him her plan to return to their own century.

"I'm remembering those loons of yours," Duguay said suddenly to Mrs. G.

She blinked at him. "My loons?"

Yes, Dani thought. Mrs. G's loons. Gwen's loons. She hugged herself, looking at Duguay, and hoping, hoping.

"They must have been a long way away from the ship," Josh said. "Did anybody see them?"

Dani looked at him blankly, and then she remembered. Josh only knew about the Arctic loons, not the loons on Gwen's lake. She searched Duguay's face anxiously. Which loons had he meant, when he said he was remembering them?

"Do you think we'll have a better chance of seeing them from the dinghy?" Duguay asked Mrs. G cheerfully, seeming not to notice how carefully Dani was watching him and listening. "Loons swim, don't they? They don't just fly?"

Mrs. G looked surprised. "Yes, they swim. They're divers, you know. For fish. They eat them. I didn't know you were interested in loons. I thought oil was the only thing in the Arctic that mattered to you."

"Oil matters," he said very seriously. "Of course it matters." His voice changed, went suddenly light. "But there's nothing more important than loons, is there?"

167

Mrs. G peered at him uncertainly. Then she shook her head and turned to the children. "Be good, you four," she said, frowning.

"The girls will show you where the North Pole is, Joshua," Duguay said, signaling to a sailor who was standing nearby.

"*They'll* show us!" Josh repeated. "But weren't we—?"

Mrs. G said, "Hurry with your experiments, Josh. I don't know how much time you're going to have, and I won't have you hanging on here inconveniencing anyone once Mr. Duguay and I are finished."

"Don't worry about that," Duguay said. "I don't think we're going to finish things all that quickly. I imagine you've got hundreds of legal precedents to explain to me —and then I've got to explain things to you, too. There's money invested here. A lot of money. And most of it isn't mine. One way or another, I expect we'll be days, discussing things."

"You faxed me that we'd only have a few hours together," Mrs. G said, a little breathlessly.

"I think that was a bit hasty on my part. Negotiations this important take time."

Mrs. G raised her brows at him. "At least now you're calling them 'negotiations,'" she said. "They were only 'discussions,' before. Does that mean you're willing to—?" She broke off. He was raising his own brows in return. "Of course," she said. "We'll talk about it on the puffhover."

"It *was* your choice," Duguay said. "Shall we go?"

They turned away, keeping pace with each other down the deck.

"So you got away with another one, eh, tweenie?" Karl said to Sara. "If that isn't just typical. Break a pendant, make a friend. Makes perfect sense to me."

Dani waited for the explosion. It didn't come. Sara smiled. "What friend? You?"

"Give me a break!"

"He means Mrs. G," Josh said gravely.

Sara smiled again. "I guess I knew that, Josh. Maybe."

Karl groaned exaggeratedly. "Come on, Josh, let's get out of here."

"Equipment," Josh said.

While the boys had their backs turned, Sara went very casually over to the spot on the deck that had been lightly chalked with an X to mark the North Pole. With the toe of one shoe she scuffed it out. "No point letting them have it for free," she said to Dani.

Dani grinned, then laughed aloud as Sara grabbed her around the waist and whirled her into a jig. "We're back, Dani," Sara said breathlessly. "Thanks to you, we're really, really back! Oh, you have no idea how good it feels to be *me* again!"

"I think I do," Dani said.

To touch someone and to know you were touched back. To hear your own voice and know it was heard. To *matter*. Yes, she thought she knew how good Sara felt.

They turned to watch Mrs. G and Duguay heading through the door that led to the staircase. They were still side by side, but some distance apart. "Will he give in to her?" Sara asked.

Dani shook her head. "I don't know. I just don't know."

"Days here, he said," Sara muttered. She looked over her shoulder at the boys, who were already coming back, lugging the sack of clocks. Her hand gripped her pendant.

"I suppose we do have to tell them where the North Pole is?" Dani said.

169

"Eventually, I guess. If we don't, someone else will. Anyway, what does it matter? I think it'll be fun to watch them try to time travel, without my pendant."

"You don't think a clock could—?"

"No way," Sara said confidently. Dani frowned. Sara looked at her, then frowned herself. Carefully, even uncertainly, she asked, "Do you?"

"No. No, I suppose not."

Sara smiled. "Good."

"So is this the North Pole?" Josh asked, dumping the sack of clocks onto the deck beside them.

Sara pursed her lips at Dani. "I suppose we could tell them, if they promise not to call us 'tweenie brains' anymore," she said.

"I suppose," Dani agreed.

"And maybe if they let us help with their experiment . . ."

"And if they make the meals for the next few days, too . . ."

"Couple of morons," Karl said disgustedly. "Who needs them? The captain'll tell us where the North Pole is."

"Right," Josh said.

They marched off. Sara hooted jeeringly after them. Dani looked at her. She seemed just the same as she always had, her friend Sara with the laughing green eyes and fierce temper and her way of taking charge and making everything an adventure. But she wasn't the same. She had been inside Gwen, inside her own grandmother. She had changed.

What else would Sara be, when time was finished with her?

What would any of them be?

170

Dani went over to the rail, wondering if Duguay and Mrs. G were out in the dinghy yet. But there was nothing to see except the waves tossing, wild and free. The wind carried with it a smell like warm salt, like storm, like the horse Thunder. A moon over a crystal lake, Dani thought, music playing and people laughing and she herself sitting alone and invisible and perfectly at peace, with the loons calling and a dog named Shags asleep at her feet.

"Gorgeous, isn't it?" Sara asked, joining her friend at the rail.

Clouds scudded before the wind. In the distance a pair of seabirds beat their wings and tried to stay aloft. They did not call to one another, or if they did, the wind blew the sound away.

Were they loons? Dani wondered. She couldn't tell. She had never actually seen a live one, she realized suddenly. Not ever, not even in the past. Maybe she never would.

But they were here, up here in the Arctic, somewhere. Maybe that was the only thing that mattered.

Time Tw   family Tw
time Yi   family Yii

better Tw
Better Yi   good Tw

than Tw   Food
Than Yi

Because Tw   You
because Yi
Tibet Yi
Tibet Tw   You

Yougart Tw
yougart Yii
Sandwtich Tw
Sandwhich Yii